George Augustus Sala

Breakfast in Bed

Or, philosophy between the sheets

George Augustus Sala

Breakfast in Bed
Or, philosophy between the sheets

ISBN/EAN: 9783337720674

Printed in Europe, USA, Canada, Australia, Japan

Cover: Foto ©Andreas Hilbeck / pixelio.de

More available books at **www.hansebooks.com**

BREAKFAST IN BED;

OR,

PHILOSOPHY BETWEEN THE SHEETS.

A Series of Indigestible Discourses,

BY GEORGE AUGUSTUS SALA,

AUTHOR OF "TWICE ROUND THE CLOCK," "WILLIAM HOGARTH," "THE SEVEN
SONS OF MAMMON," "THE STRANGE ADVENTURES OF CAPTAIN
DANGEROUS," ETC., ETC., ETC.

———◄♦►———

BOSTON:

JAMES REDPATH, Publisher,

221 Washington Street.

1863.

TO

MY KIND DOCTOR

H. J. J.

WHO SET ME ON MY LEGS

AND

WOULD TAKE NO FEE,

I Dedicate this Book,

WRITTEN IN SICKNESS BUT REVISED IN HEALTH.

Guilford Street, Russell Square,
September, 1863.

CONTENTS.

————•••————

BREAKFAST IN BED;

OR,

PHILOSOPHY BETWEEN THE SHEETS.

———•••———

ON A REMARKABLE DRAMATIC PER-
FORMANCE.

Do you know Hircius and Spungius, servants
to Dorothea, in that curious old play by Mass-
inger, the *Virgin Martyr?* I have always looked
upon these two fellows as the perfection of
scoundrelism. To steal pence off the tray of a
blind man's dog is ordinarily esteemed the *acmé*
of baseness; but Hircius and Spungius go far
beyond this. They take the saintly Virgin's
wages, but they are bond-servants to Venus—
La Venere de' ruffiani, and to Bacchus (Bacchus
who is head warden of Vintners' Hall, ale conner,
mayor of all victualling houses; lanceprezade to
red noses and invincible Adalantado over the
armada of deep-scarleted, rubified, and carbun-
cled faces). How they drink and gorge, and

7

swear and lie, and bear false witness! When
Dorothea sends them out with meat and medi-
cines to comfort her almswomen, Hircius and
Spungius convey the cates to a receiver of stolen
goods, and spend the proceeds in foul riot.
"For blood of grapes they sell the widow's
food," and "snatch the meat out of the prison-
er's mouth" to fatten the naughty. With vile
hypocrisy they simulate devotion; but when the
meek Angelo, who is always walking about with
upturned eyes and a lighted taper, has gone on his
way, Hircius and Spungius thrust their tongues
into their cheeks, and reel into the nearest tavern, blaspheming. Finally, when Dorothea,
their mistress, their benefactress, their Saint, is
to be scourged, outraged, tortured, who but Hircius and Spungius are there to help the hangman? Faugh! There is but one merry passage
in this mournful tragedy, and that is where the
twin villains are dragged away by the heels to
the gallows.

Every man who feels strongly, and works
hard, and has made a name, and hates Rogues,
is pestered with a Hircius and a Spungius. They
begin by fawning upon and slavering him; and
when they discover that he will have none of
their lip-service, they become his enemies. With
one more ally, they would be counterparts of the
three Jews who put their three-hatted heads

together to "devise devices against Jeremiah,
and make his life a torment to him." Ever
since I laid down pencil to take up pen, I have
had my Hircius and my Spungius for ever carp-
ing, sneering, maligning, reviling. Hircius
libels me in the "Cad's Chronicle" because I have
declined to lend him three-and-sixpence; Spungius, who is reviewer-in-ordinary to the "Gutter-
blood Gazette," essays to filch from me my good
name because I would not insert his "New Scandal about Queen Elizabeth" in "Temple Bar."
Yet I honestly confess that the enmity of Hircius and Spungius does me good. It is better,
O sage, to wriggle on a cushion stuffed full of
the thorns of abuse than to rest the head on the
hop-pillow of flattery. A mongrel cur barking
at your heels is not so agreeable, but he is more
useful than a cringing Boswell. Then, again, is
there not a pleasure in taking one's traducers by
the ear, and cudgelling their bewrayed hides
with sounding thwacks? To hear Hircius howl,
to listen to Spungius as he squeals—this is sack
and sugar to one who is content to abide by the
wholesome doctrine of give and take, and who,
in return for a craven blow, can deliver the
"auctioneer" well over the face and eyes.

"Aha!" I hear Hircius and Spungius cry
when they open this sheet, and see "Breakfast
in Bed" at the head of the page. "Now we

1*

have him on the hip. Now we will gird at him,
and˙snarl, and glose, and 'make his life a torment to him.'" Yes, H. and S., so shall you do
till you swell and burst with venom, if you like
the sport. "Oho!" Hircius and Spungius continue, "Breakfast in Bed, forsooth! Here is
another sample of literary vanity. His lordship
breakfasts in bed, docs he, and not at the penny
coffee-shop? What does he condescend to take
at his breakfast? Chocolate frothed in a silver
mill? devilled kidneys, muffins, flowery pekoe,
truffled turkey, or Strasburg pie? Does he read
the 'Morning Post?'" (Yes, he does; and a
capital paper it is, with columns inexorably
closed against Hircian and Spungian contribu-
tions.) "Does he subsequently rise, don a brocaded dressing-gown, and, with a golden pen, on
violet-tinted paper, set down the thoughts that
have flitted through his mind at breakfast-time?
Or, does his Ineffability (and be hanged to his
impudence!) have a rosewood writing-desk inlaid
with ivory (Mechi and Bazin, makers) brought
to his bedside, and deposited on his pink silk
quilted counterpane, while a trembling slave
holds the standish? Or, perhaps, we shall be
favored with a description of the bedchamber on
the model—he is an inveterate plagiarist—of
Xavier de Maistre's *Voyage autour de ma Cham-
bre.* Now for a broker's inventory of the furni-

ture: chairs, washhand-stand, tiger-skin rug, and adjoining bath-room. Oh, be joyful; let us say grace, my brother, for anon we shall be full of meat. The old, old Galimatias is coming. The old conceit, ignorance, fragments of slangy French, scraps of bad Latin, wiredrawn descriptions, interminable digressions, and affected verbiage. And this wretched imitation of the immortal 'Roundabout Papers' he calls 'Breakfast in Bed.' Breakfast in bed, quotha! Why not Breakfast on a doorstep, Breakfast in the workhouse, Breakfast in gaol?"

Well, all may be on the cards; for the life of mortal man is full of strange vicissitudes. Meanwhile I am content to Breakfast in Bed. Do You, my reader, want a reason for a decidedly indolent and perhaps unhealthy habit? You should have a hundred, were you so minded. I breakfast in bed because I like it; because I am much given to sitting up all night, with cats, and owls, and friends, and books, and things; because I am generally very tired when I go to bed, and my poor feet require rest as well as my poor head; because a cup of tea taken between the sheets tastes more sweetly to me than the family souchong on the ground-floor; because I am much given to quarrelling with my bread-and-butter at breakfast-time—and, alone, in bed there are but two parties to the quarrel instead

of three or four; because there is a bell close to
my hand, which I can pull viciously when I
choose; because one can get through the perusal
of six daily papers much better in bed than in
an arm-chair; and finally, because when in bed
in the fresh morning, and wide awake, not in
the incoherence of drowsiness, one can think,
plot, devise, arrange, decide upon the momentous Yea, the irrevocable No; bid farewell to the
evil, welcome the good and rise a new man.

Never mind what my sleeping apartment is
like. Damask-hung four-poster, ceiled with
plate-glass; feather-bed and down pillow, or
iron pallet, with straw paillasse and hard-
stuffed bolster—what does it matter? I ask not
Hircius and Spongius to what twopenny-rope
their hammocks are hung pending the final *sus.*
per coll. How many pairs of boots are there in
the dressing-room? Do I urticate my back hair
with two brushes (ivory-backed)? Have I any
Ess. Bouquet, Rondeletia, or Toilet Vinegar on
the dressing-table? All these are things of little
moment. Suffice it to say that the windows are
open from the top, that there is no looking-glass
in the room—for this reason, that most men
have an invincible propensity for looking at their
tongue the first thing in the morning, and when
you look at your tongue you can't help looking
at your face; and then comes the cold shudder

when you discover that you are a night older, and that gray hair number nineteen has just put in an appearance. Stay, there is one other circumstance which I may mention in connection with my domestic arrangements. On the wall opposite my bed hangs, neatly framed, an old Dutch Engraving of the martyrdom of some five hundred saints, who suffered in the persecutions of the Roman Emperors from Valerian to Maxentius. There they are, being fried, grilled, boiled, roasted, barbecued, flayed alive, burnt, steamed, whipped, pinched, hanged, decapitated, baked, drowned, minced, scolloped, hewn in pieces, sawn asunder, impaled, broken on the wheel, and flung to wild beasts. A lively composition, with a long epigraph in Dutch, beginning " *Het Martelen der bloedgetuigen de onder der Vervolging der Roomse Keisers voer de Waarheid des Evangeliums,*" and so forth! I like to look at this sanguinolent old print, first, in complacency for being in bed, in Bloomsbury, in the Queen's peace, with the breakfast things coming jangling upstairs on the tray—Ha!˙ another breakage at that unlucky second-pair landing; next, in gratitude remembering that the five hundred persons here represented were cruelly done to death because they presumed to differ in matters of conscience from the " Roomse Keisers ;" and, thank God! no King or Kaiser

nowadays dare so much as pinch an Englishman's little finger for what he writes or speaks
according to his conscience.

Cannot one get up a little Philosophy between
the Sheets this fine rainy morning? Here are
the Newspapers. Surely some texts must turn
up in those extensive, close-printed, loose-medi-
tated columns. In the advertisements always
there is a mine of philosophy; but they always
detain the "Times" Supplement down-stairs—I
presume with a hankering after the Births, Mar-
riages, and Deaths, the abandoned Initials who
have run away from home, and the Bank an-
nouncements of unclaimed stock. There is none
standing in *my* name, I am sure. Here are the
telegrams—Reuter's hottest? The Tuileries compliment Turin. Do they? The Reichsrath? No;
it's the Landtag. Stay, it's the council of the
nobility of the government of Tamboff, who
have been memorializing somebody about something. Indeed! Montenegro. Where is Montenegro? There is no use in consulting the map;
for has not a great authority informed us that all
maps professing to give a projection of any places
out of the British Dominions are simply impostures? The Turks have taken Spuz, and are
marching on Cettigne. Much good may it do
them! Another dreadful murder. There is
always another dreadful murder. Infanticide.

Ditto. Swindling extraordinary; more garotte robberies; death through crinoline; Lord John Manners on agricultural prizes; Mr. Henley on laborers' cottages; Mr. Disraeli on himself; " consols opened heavily "—did they? state of trade; suicide; destitution; another awful fire. Well, I do not see that the world has altered its ordinary jog-trot since yesterday,—since 2,190,000 yesterdays, more or less. We are still laboring, groaning, crashing in M. Victor Hugo's dark tunnel; and I for one am choked with the engine's ever-belching smoke, and deafened by the rattle and roar; and they don't give us lights in the second-class carriages; and thrusting my head out of the window, at the risk of having it (the head) knocked off, I can see no glimmer of the luminous point which is so visible to M. Hugo's eagle eye—the happy valley; the promised land; the bright terminus—Canaan.

Here are leading articles galore. "It was once wittily remarked by Rochefoucault."— *Connu.* "The Fabian policy of General McClellan,"—I have seen that before. "Those whom the gods are resolved to destroy they first deprive of reason; and the conduct of the Indian government with reference to the Gwalior bungalows, the farming of mofussils to Kansamahs, and the breach of Sudder Adawlut towards the ryots of the Himalayan compounds"—Very clever and ex-

haustive, I have no doubt; but my acquaintance
with Hindostan stops at curried lobster, and Indian politics are to me among the *cosas de
España.*

I just glance at the theatrical advertisements
above the leaders. My eye lights on the un-
varying staple of the bill of fare at the Haymarket. *Our American Cousin,* of course. Tremendous and continued success of Mr. Sothern
as *Lord Dundreary.* Why, let me collect my
thoughts. Where was I last night? whom did I
meet? with whom did I quarrel? which are synonymous terms. Why, I went to the Theatre
Royal Haymarket, and paid for my admission—
at least, somebody else paid for me, the free list
being suspended, and orders hopelessly unattain-
able; and I saw Mr. Sothern in *Lord Dundreary,* and I have seen him twice within as
many weeks.

I don't often go to the play. It is too good
for the likes of me. I envy the people who seem
to enjoy the performance, which wearies and stu-
pifies me. I am restless and uneasy; long for
the green curtain to descend, and for the festoons
of brown holland to envelope the boxes. I never
sat out a theatrical performance without wishing,
not that the roof might fall in, and the chande-
lier tumble into the pit—for those accidents
would hurt my brethren below—but that the

stage-manager would step forward and inform the audience that the French had landed, or that a blue monkey was standing on his head on the summit of Bow-church steeple, or that Captain Fowke's brick barn at South Kensington had caught fire: anything sensational, in fact, to put a stop to the mummery on the stage and clear the house. I had not, before I went to see *Lord Dundreary*, been inside the Haymarket theatre for years. I remember the last time well; the pit black with paying play-goers' heads, the boxes radiant with famous men and fair women, and one old man on the stage, white-bearded, straw-bedecked, babbling to his Fool about his daughter's ingratitude. *Vidi tantum.* I have seen William Charles Macready in *King Lear;* and after that wondrous impersonation, the rant and buffoonery of the modern stage disgust a dull man somewhat. Exult not, my Hircius and Spungius; I am not about to descant on the glorious old days of the drama—on Young and Charles Kemble, whom I have seen—on *the* Kean, whom I never saw—on "Jack Bannister, sir," who died years before I was born.

And let me tell Mr. John Baldwin Buckstone, whom I have known, admired, and respected for very many years—who has been, I am proud to say, from the first, a subscriber to this Magazine, that he is very much mistaken if he thinks I am

about to puff either Mr. Sothern or himself. No,
J. B. B., perpend. You may cut off with ruthless
excision your subscription to *T. B.*, but you shall
listen to the impartial critic now Breakfasting in
Bed. You may strike, but you shall hear.

Some kind, despotic friends I am happy to
possess were good enough, lately, to take me to
the Exhibition (where I had never been, of my
own motion, since the opening day) and to feed
me on macaroni dressed in the Neapolitan fashion, with tomatoes, and to give me some grouse,
and some selzer and sillery, and other nice things,
which cast a sunshine on the shady walks of life,
and to tell me that three front seats had been
secured a week before at the Haymarket, and
that I was to go, *en sandwich*, and see *Lord
Dundreary*. I protested; but in vain. I pleaded
my engagements, the printer's devil of *T. B.*, my
incapacity to appreciate the drama, my aching
head, and those perennial poor feet. All remon-
strances I found unavailing; and ten minutes
before the termination of a very stupid farce, I
found myself in the first agonies of that cramp
which is the lot of all who occupy front rows at
an English theatre.

It is not, I conceive, necessary that I should
describe the plot and incidents of the piece, entitled *Our American Cousin*, and which is called
a Comedy. This much, however, I may say, that

it is, as regards construction, dialogue and intrigue, about as much a comedy as I am a Dutchman. As comedies go, however, I suppose that it is received as something quite in the style of Sheridan or Mrs. Inchbald. There is plenty of " broad fun " in it, which may be said to be analogous with "Broad church," *i. e.*, no fun at all Is it.funny for the " tag " to the first act to depend on a Yankee pulling the string of a shower-bath, and bellowing beneath the cascade ; or for the wind-up of the second to turn on the popping of a champagne-cork and the casting of an effervescing jet over *Lord Dundreary?* These funniments remind one of the old " real water " effects of Sadler's Wells. The fun of Mr. Buckstone appearing in the costume of the Ancient Order of Foresters, dilating on the pleasant odor of the back hair of the young lady he is hugging, and of his mixing sherry-cobblers and brandy-cocktails in an English drawing-room, I cannot discover. But all this must be funny, you see, because the public roar with laughter at every feat of mountebank horse-play ; and whatever is, you know, is right.

Although Mr. Buckstone's *Asa Trenchard* does not in the slightest degree resemble either a Northern or a Southern American, it is undeniably a very droll performance. But then Mr. Buckstone would be sure to make you laugh

were he playing the part, say of a Mute, or of
Hamlet Prince of Denmark, or of Grim Death
himself. He makes the most of an unnatural
and ungrateful *rôle*, manifestly written *down* by
a bad dramatist to suit the morbid vanity of a
Bowery audience—or wherever else in Bragga-
dociodom the thing was primarily played. Indeed, the whole "comedy" bears evident signs
of being written to order, and with the view of
"cracking up" the most conceited people in the
world. The quasi-American from Vermont is
made chivalrous, generous, self-sacrificing, even
to lighting his cigar with the document which
assures him the possession of large property;
while, of the two most salient English gentlemen
represented, one is a "bloated aristocrat" of a
Baronet, hopelessly in debt, the other a vapid,
brainless nobleman. All the types of English
character, save *Florence* and *Mary* (who is to
have the signal honor of marrying the Yankee),
are absurd and repulsive. The butler is a mon-
strosity of malaspirated H's; the dairyman who
brings the letters is a cringing fawner; the law-
yer (the villain of the piece) is a thief, and his
clerk a drunkard. *Captain De Boots* is a fool
and nothing more; and *Mrs. Mountchessington*
has the manners of a charwoman, and sells her
daughters to the highest bidders. This, I suppose, is English Society. Is it? I am sure I

don't know. I don't go into society myself;—
and, my dear, I have rung twice for another
lump of sugar; and to-morrow being Sunday we
will go to the Foundling Chapel, and be thankful for all things.

I look upon the *Lord Dundreary* of Mr.
Sothern as a most finished, ingenious, and amaz-
ingly well-sustained delineation of a character
he has undeniably originated:—that of a well-
dressed but grotesque imbecile. It is easy to see
directly he comes on the stage the man is a
thorough actor. Like Mr. Fechter, he is never
idle; his by-play is always exquisite, never
obtrusive. Many comedians, when they have
done mouthing what is set down for them, sub-
side at once into gawky inertia; and because
they are no longer near the footlights, think that
they have a right to twiddle their thumbs, to
yawn, to stand on one leg, to gossip with their
compeers, or to gaze vacantly at the wings.
They are just like the Marionettes you see at
Genoa: one moment full of spasmodic action,
and the next flaccid and powerless, with their
heads on one side, their backbones apparently
drawn out, and propped against the wing. With
Mr. Sothern it is entirely different. You never
see too much of him, when in comparative
repose; but you may be always sure that he is
doing the right thing in the right place. He

dresses in wonderfully good taste. His costumes
(with one exception, which I shall notice presently) are true to the character which, otherwise, he so often falsifies. His face is mar-
vellously "made-up;" his management of an
eye-glass as dexterous as Perea Nena's management of a fan. He cannot unfold a pocket-
handkerchief, open a letter, put on a pair of
gloves, cross his legs, or pull his moustaches,
without showing you that he has made those
seemingly petty details the matter of careful and
artistic study. Finally, to sum up his good qualities, he appears to be an admirable mimic, and
imitates very successfully the drawl, the lisp, and
the stutter, which he has turned to such famous
account. He is the more entitled to praise for
his powers of mimicry, as the tones of his natural
voice, when heard from time to time, have a
harsh and unpleasant twang, suggesting to those
who hear him that *Asa Trenchard* in his hands,
or rather in his mouth, would be much more a
lifelike performance than is the Yankee of Mr.
Buckstone.

And the *per contrâ. Is* there anything to be
said on the other side ? Can anything, without
malice or hypercriticism, be set down in depre-
ciation of an actor who has taken the town by
storm, who for months has crammed the Haymarket to the very ceiling, whose photograph is

in every shop-window, whose name the theme of
every drawing-room conversation, who has won
colossal notoriety for himself, and has made a
handsome fortune—for his manager? I think
that there is a great deal to be said on the other
side, and I mean to say it plainly, but temperately. First, however, let me express my
opinion that the responsibility of the blemishes
to which I am about to call attention lies at the
door, not of Mr. Sothern, not even at that of the
playwright, who originally gave only the sketchy
skeleton of a part which Mr. Sothern has clothed
in such a vascular manner, but at the door of his
audience. The gallery roar at him because he is
full of laughable absurdities. The pit are de-
lighted with him, because the pittites are mostly
simple-minded country-folks, who know no more
of the habits and manners of a live lord than
they do of the private life of a hippopotamus.
The stuck-up middle-classes in the boxes praise
his impersonation as " so delightfully true to
nature," because they themselves have rarely the
opportunity of meeting with the aristocracy ; and
because Mr. Sothern's *Dundreary* is the caricature
of a caricature, the exaggeration of the sham copy
they are themselves acquainted with—the Government clerks and sucking bankers and stock-
brokers' sons, who dress in an *outré* manner,
know the outside of all the clubs, walk arm

linked four abreast in Rotten Row, and fancy
themselves "swells." Mr. John Leech, even,
who ought to know his swell by heart, has blun-
dered in seizing upon the *outer Dundreary* as
the type of the inner exquisite; and the thousands who pin their faith to the social sketches
in "Punch" are content to believe that if Mr.
Leech, like Mr. Lincoln, "puts down his foot"
on *Lord Dundreary* being identical with the real
swells, with my Lord Tomnoddy, and Lord Fre-
derick Verisopht, and—swells of swells!—the
Marquis of Farintosh and the Honorable Percy
Popjoy—Mr. Leech must be right, and no dog
must dare bark at Sir Oracle. But I pass from
assertion to proof. When so much is said about
"life-like portraiture," and something "delightfully true to nature," it behooves me to show in
what manner Mr. Sothern sins against verisimi-
litude in the character he assumes. I am inclined, first, to think that *Lord Dundreary's*
appearance in brilliantly-dyed black hair, moustache, and whiskers is, artistically considered, a
mistake. Nine-tenths of our English swells are
tawny. Old swells use hair-dye (on the employment of which by *Dundreary* part of the plot
of this precious piece turns); young swells
never. I will, however, pass this by, as now
and then one meets a phenomenally sable swell;
only Mr. Sothern "makes up" so very darkly as

to appear almost oriental. A much more reprehensible solecism is his first entrance in an elaborately embroidered dressing-gown. Since when has such a careless style of attire been tolerated, even in the case of a nobleman, in the house of an English baronet, and in the presence of ladies and gentlemen who are all in walking dress? Again, the real "swell," donkey as he frequently may be, would never be so positively rude and unmannerly to ladies as Mr. Sothern is. He might be lazy, lounging and limp; but, as the English swell can generally ride, drive, and fence very well, he is hardly ever awkward. It is the perfectly calm self-possession and the languid politeness of the swell that give him so unmistakeable a stamp. Mr. Sothern is always committing blunders, tumbling over settees, knocking over music-stools, or frightening old ladies out of their wits. He has not been three minutes on the stage, before he turns his back on the lady with whom he is conversing. I do not object to his speaking of *Mrs. Mountchessington*, in an under tone, as "a d—d stupid old woman," for I am afraid that the swells are much given to quiet profanity; but I do object to his jogging that lady in the stomacher and hustling her about the room:—I object simply for this reason, that if any *Lord Dundreary* adopted such a course of conduct in any English

2

drawing-room, he would infallibly be kicked down-stairs by the host. Of Mr. Sothern's drawl I have already expressed my admiration. His lisp is also very good, and is not offensive, for the more imbecile among the swells do imitate or acquire by habit a lisp. But that part of an actor's great reputation should rest upon his mimicry of so painful, lamentable, and repulsive a physical imperfection as *stammering*, strikes me as being very disgusting. A lisp is a slight matter: the stammerer and stutterer must be reckoned among the Almighty's afflicted creatures. If corporeal ailments are to be made the subject of "life-like portraiture" in "comedy," we shall have one actor famous for his wonderful delineation of the ringworm, another made famous through his stage-photography of a harelip, and a third gain renown for his curious copy of club-foot. In fact, Mr. Sothern very nearly approaches a parody of the last-named defect, in the shape of a hop, or "kick in his gallop," which a *young English lady* accounts for by saying that my Lord has been advised to run, and that he is doing his running by instalments. This young lady, *Florence* (very charmingly played by Mrs. Charles Young), also ridicules *Lord Dundreary* to his face for saying "widdle," instead of "riddle," an exercise of sarcastic humor I did not hitherto know to be habitual in polite society.

Much of Mr. Sothern's popularity rests on the incoherent nonsense he talks, and the idiotic *non sequiturs* in which he revels. The confusion arising from his utter want of the faculty of reason is certainly very amusing. For instance, when he tries to count his fingers and toes, and discovers that he has eleven of each; when he sticks up one thumb to represent his mother, and another for his brother Sam's mother, until he gets into a haze between the two, and wonders who the d—l (he is nearly always swearing) his mother can be, it is impossible to avoid shouting with laughter. I wonder, supposing my friend Mr. Nicholas were to send me up a Born Idiot from the admirable Asylum at Earlswood, and I were to try to procure him an engagement at the Haymarket, whether the drivelling balderdash of the poor creature would excite the risibility of a highly cultivated audience? Many of Mr. Sothern's *non sequiturs* are droll enough; but they are not new. The enumeration of the fingers and toes is as old as the hills, and has made many generations of chaw-bacons grin when performed by Mr. Merryman in front of a booth at the fair. The transposition of proverbs in which *Lord Dundreary* delights is equally venerable; and I had the pleasure of hearing the famous hotch-potch of "the early bird knows his own father," and "a wise child picks up the worm" (if that be the precise formula of the nonsense), from the mouth of an English clown, in the circus at Copenhagen, and in the year of grace 1856. Indeed, the majority of the jokes smell of the sawdust, and have been heard over and over again at Astley's. The more refined witticisms are drawn from other sources. The perpetual reference to "some other fellah" is only a paraphrase of the "any other man" of the nigger stump-orator at the music-halls; and the joint-stool conversation between *Dundreary* and *Georgiana* at the Dairy-farm is not very skilfully copied from a wonderful bit of inane chit-chat in one of Mrs. German Reed's earlier entertainments. If I remember correctly, it hinged upon an asinine young gentleman's asking a lady whether she liked cheese, or whether, if she had a brother, she thought that *he* would like that caseous delicacy.

Do I blame, do I quarrel with Mr. Sothern for making himself the mouthpiece of all this bald buffoonery? Not in the least. I only quarrel with the silly and depraved people who persist in crying up as a "life-like portraiture" and "as delightfully true to nature" what might just as well be assumed to be the likeness of Beau Tibbs or Beau Brummel, as that of an English aristocrat of the nineteenth century. I dare say the Americans admired *Lord Dundreary* hugely. To

the greater number of those who flock to see Mr.
Sothern in England, he would be quite as welcome if he wore a sky-blue coat, a false nose,
and a pink wig. , We want quantity now-a-days,
not quality, in our humor. The " Perfect Cure"
has been an immense success; so has " In the
Strand, in the Strand ;" and if anybody will tell
me the real gist of those celebrated " comic"
songs, I will give him any number of post obits,
my MS. notes for the history of Merry Andrews,
and a live guinea-pig.

I apprehend that Mr. Sothern came to play
this part in England in perfect good faith, and
that he became a hero without being aware of it.
Dundreary had had a tremendous run in America; why shouldn't it go down in England?
Mr. Sothern has been, I believe, resident for
many years in the United States and in the Colo-
nies. It is not very probable that he could have
enjoyed many opportunities of studying the peculiarities of the class of whom *Lord Dundreary*
is erroneously supposed to be the type. He
created the part, or at least filled it up from a
mere vague outline. He saw how it would
square with his own particular notion of humor,
how he could adapt it to his own idiosyncrasy.
He has been triumphantly successful in the pro-
duction of a "life-like portraiture," not of a
dandy Lord, but of an Eccentric. I don't deny

that there may be a *Dundreary* or two wander-
ing up and down society ; but I utterly repudiate
the theory accepted by the public, and endorsed
by the powerful pencil of Mr. Leech, that Mr.
Sothern's *Dundreary* is the representative of a
class in the community. The Haymarket actor
has, however, succeeded, perhaps unconsciously,
in naturalizing in England a character who, for
many years, has been highly popular on the
French stage. I mean the traditional *Jocrisse.*
The late Mr. Kenney gave a very humorous notion of him in the *Billy Lackaday* of *Sweet-
hearts and Wives ;* but *Lord Dundreary* is a
thorough Anglicised *Jocrisse.* When this droll
imbecile is sent for a quart of oil he holds out
his cap, which contains a pint. When asked
how he will carry the other pint, he turns the
cap inside out. His master tells him to count
the chickens, and he says that he has reckoned
them all up except one, which ran about so that
he couldn't count it. He digs a hole in the
ground ; and when asked how he means to get
rid of the earth thrown up, replies, " Put it in
that hole, of course." He asks for some stale
bread instead of new, at dinner, and being told
that there is none, desires that some stale bread
may be baked. He sees a fresh salmon at the
fishmonger's, and announces his intention to save
up his pocket-money until he can buy it. The

cat jumps on to the bird-cage, claws the canary out, and eats it. Hearing his mistress coming, *Jocrisse* thrusts the cat into the cage, and declares that the canary is quite safe, because it is *là-dedans*, pointing to the imprisoned felina. There are *Jocrisses*, under various names, at Naples, at Palermo, at Madrid, at Constantinople, at Moscow, as I dare say there were likewise in old Rome and old Athens. Who doesn't know the old, old incongruity of the traveller who exclaimed, " They may well call this place Stoney Stratford, for I have been most terribly bitten by fleas!" What is that but a Dundrearyism pure and simple? The town has chosen to go mad after the English *Jocrisse ;* and the town, I suppose, is perfectly right. Long live Lord Dundreary at the Haymarket, Blondin on the high rope, Léotard on the *trapéze*, the Perfect Cure, The Strand, the Strand! and the Benizoug-zoug Arabs! If I say that this vulgar farrago at the Haymarket, libellously called a comedy, and this clever droll, who has so successfully moulded it to his own purpose, made me think with shame and sorrow of the days when WRENCH, STRICKLAND, FARREN, MATHEWS, VESTRIS, GLOVER, NISBETT, trod its boards, and BUCKSTONE gave us Englishmen to the life, and not galvanized travesties of Yankees,—what am I but a jaundiced and splenetic croaker? The

drama is dead. Hurrah for "sensations," comic
or tragic! The theatrical city of Paris is not
free from similar crazes. All Paris crowded five-
and-forty years ago to see *Les Anglaises pour
rire;* thirty years ago to see *Passé Minuit;*
twenty years ago to see *Le Thé chez Madame
Gibou;* ten years ago to see a performer who
had, in his way, as great a specialty as Mr.
Sothern. His name was Joseph Kelm; and he
created a furore by singing a comic song called
Le Sire de Framboisy, in which there was a truly
Dundrearyish line, telling how the Sire cut off
his wife's head *d'un coup de son fusil:*—with a
musket shot. But it strikes me that all the extra-
vaganzas I have named ran their course at little
trumpery Boulevard theatres; and that the hu-
mors of M. Joseph Kelm were confined to the
Funambules or the Folies Nouvelles. The *Sire
de Framboisy* did not invade the chosen homes
of comedy. He did not claim a triumph at the
Théâtre Français.

Yes: there certainly was either too much cay-
enne-pepper, or too much Worcestershire sauce
with—never mind what? the kidneys, the grilled
haddock, the devilled fowl,—anything you like.
Breakfast is over; hot water arrives; and Black
Care stands over against the shaving-glass and
scowls at the shaver.

ON A LITTLE BOY GOING TO SCHOOL.

SHORTLY after eight o'clock every morning a little boy comes into the room where I Breakfast in Bed—a very little boy, not so high as the counterpane of the couch, and clad in a little suit of gray frieze. He passes to a little corner appointed to him, partially disrobes himself, and, with a very grave and magisterial air, washes his little hands and face. That he has just partaken of a cold bath is patent from the fluffy appearance of his wet hair, a slight shiver which sometimes pervades his frame, and the occasional trace of a half-dried tear on his dumpling face, which tear, I am led, not irrationally, to believe, has a direct connection with sundry early morning howlings, sometimes audible to me from the upper regions. I will not do servant-maids the injustice to suppose that they wilfully and designedly rub yellow soap or the hard corners of towels into little boys' eyes; but I well remember what tortures I used to undergo in the tub, where I was washed against my will, and was of the same opinion still that the making of dirtpies was preferable. "*Laissez-moi jouer dans cette belle*

2*

boue !" the Emperor Napoleon is reported to have
said, pointing to a magnificent puddle visible
from the palace window at the Hague, when his
mamma asked him what he would like for a new-
year's gift. It is a dreadful thing to be exposed,
weak and defenceless, in a Tub : yourself, *all face*
as the Red Indians have it, and in that smooth
shiny condition at once a prey and a temptation
to the horny palm of a quick-tempered nursery-
maid. However, as this little boy is to many intents and purposes master of the house in which
he resides, I don't think that he suffers more than
moderate tribulations in connection with the tub.
At all events, his sorrows are over when he comes
down to me. It is plain that the face-and-hands-
laving he goes through in my presence is in his
mind a pastime, not an irksome task. It is a
sight to see him immerse his small paws in the
water, demurely and decorously at first, but grad-
ually ceding to an incontrollable impulse to
splash. At 7.30 years of age what rich mines of
happiness are there in making a mess! His per-
formances with the nail brush are wonderful; but
they are ornamental, not useful, the little boy
having very little nails to speak of. He goes
nevertheless through all the traditional etiquette
of "making himself tidy," and in so doing reminds me irresistibly of a kitten of which I have
been lately bereaved, and now of a rabbit spruc-

ing himself up in the presence of a boa-constrict-
or, unconscious that the monster in the blanket
is about to breakfast upon him—as I, the domestic boa (or bore), propose to do presently upon
the little boy—not truly to the extent of devour-
ing him, but merely with a view to making him
my theme for half-a-dozen pages or so. He proceeds to comb the little auburn mop which sur-
rounds his head like a carelessly-drawn nimbus,
and makes about eight partings in indifferent
directions in lieu of one. All of these *faits et
gestes* are, I need scarcely observe, perfunctory,
and merely devised for the purpose of "putting
him in the way of things." Anon he will be
made spruce and tidy by other hands.

He has been by no means silent during these
varied operations. He has on entering bidden
me good morning, and "passed the time of day,"
as it is colloquially termed. He has likewise, in
the course of about ten minutes, asked me about
fifty questions. Some of these are, I must own,
embarrassing. I admit that I am shaky as to my
geography, and that I do not know the exact distance from London to Turkey in Asia. I con-
cede the general propositions started by the little
boy that Russia looks very big on the map, and
that it is a long way to Spain; but when he proceeds to cross-question me as to Sweden and Denmark, and generally to retail to me so much as

he remembers of his last oral lesson from Miss
Mangnall of the Preparatory Establishment for
Young Gentlemen, I take refuge on my deaf side,
hum something from the *Trovatore*, or artfully
start a fresh topic of conversation. But I am
proud to say that, however close I may be run, I
never take refuge in the time-dishonored evasion
that "little boys ought not to ask questions"—
than which I think there is no crueller, stupider,
or wickeder shield to your own ignorance and
bar to another's enlightenment, extant. I remember that, as a child, I used to be beaten for
being inquisitive; and I know that by this time
I should be begging my bread and not earning
it did I not pass the major portion of my time
in asking questions. Good Heavens! what would
become of the world if little boys were not permitted to ask questions? When grown up, they
would be at grass with Nebuchadnezzar, and
have one life with the beasts of the field. Yet
may there be something belonging to the inner
mystery of our being in this prohibition of know-
ledge-seeking to infancy. How we lie and lie to
children almost until they become men and women! How sedulously we keep secret the pri-
mary things we know, and yet are so ready to
impart the knowledge of that we know nothing
of—the Devil! The upas shadow of the Tree
of Knowledge of Good and Evil is upon us, and

we dread to drag the bantlings into it. For who has puberty and reason but knows that he is perpetually pursued by a sphynx propounding the unanswerable enigma, "What is Life?"—failing to answer which the sphynx devours him and he dies?

There are other ways in which the little boy's interrogatories are perplexing. When he comes up again while I am breakfasting, to bid me good-bye before proceeding to school, he sometimes asks "why I have not eaten all my bread-and-butter?" I may answer, "Because I have a headache." He may resume, "But why have I a headache?" To this my response may be, "Because I was out very late." "But why was I out very late?" I may reply, "Because I was detained at the office correcting proofs." Here I have the little boy on the hip. The correction of proofs is as yet a profound mystery to him, and his inquisitive faculty does not at present extend beyond "why." When he is eight, he will begin to ask "what" and "where." When he is a man, he will ask "who."

He is a condescending little boy, not at all proud, and is glad to act as a species of domestic commissionnaire, fetching and carrying such small matters as letters, newspapers, anchovy paste up and down stairs. He is told that his performance of these little offices "saves the ser-

vants' legs;" and I think that willingness and
courtesy on the part of children save not only the
servants' legs but their tempers likewise, and that
to teach a child to say "if you please" whenever he asks a retainer for anything, is almost as
useful as a lecture upon geography. Have you
not known a little boy the pest and nuisance of
and entire house, and cursed by the subordinates
he is permitted to bully? The "bloated aristocracy" set us a shining example in this respect.
Who keep their servants longest—for two generations often—and leave them legacies when they
die? The haughtiest nobles, who, as a class, are
uniformly courteous and urbane to their domestics. Who change their servants once a month—
once a week sometimes—and are for ever wrang-
ling and jangling with them? The ignorant,
envious, selfish, stuck-up classes. A little boy
tyrannizing over a servant is, next to a little boy
lending out his pocket-money at interest, the un-
loveliest of human sights.

And so this quiet little creature walks and talks
in his Lilliputian way about the house, until it is
time for him to go to school. It is the privilege
of the cook to convey him thither, and to fetch
him when school is over; and although I think
he knows the way to Miss Mangnall's Preparatory Establishment in Great Pinnock Street much
better than Cook (who is from the country) knows

it, he very cheerfully acquiesces in the arrangement as part of his state of nonage and pupilage.
He would as soon think of proceeding to school
alone as of smoking a meerschaum-pipe on his
way thither. He thoroughly accepts and understands his position as a very little boy. Now and
then, when I am dawdling over a book, and he,
playing with his few toys, is adjuring imaginary
horses, locomotive engines, or railway porters "to
come up," or marshalling mystical armies into
position, I catch a shrewd-glance in the corners
of his eyes directed towards me, as though he
were thinking, "I dare say that I am talking
nonsense; but why shouldn't I talk it, being such
a very little boy!" Children have a wonderful
power of conjuring up invisible interlocutors;
and I think I would much sooner hear a little boy
"playing at being" something he is not, or conversing with a fancied playmate, than witness the
hallucination of Justice Trice in Dryden's play,
who is discovered "playing at tables with himself,
spectacles on, and a bottle and parmesan before
him," crying, "Cinq and cater: my cinq I play
here, sir; my cater here, sir. But first I'll drink
to you, sir. Upon my faith, I'll do you reason."

I have travelled about half-way through Breakfast in Bed when it is time for the little boy to
depart for school. He comes, fully equipped for
the Groves of Academe, to bid me farewell; and

although he revisits the house at midday, I see no more of him until evening, when just before dinner and his bed-time he asks me a few—say half a hundred—more questions.

I believe that in accordance with the modern formula of essay-writing I should properly cry, "*I, curre!*" to this little boy, and say something about his youth, his innocence, his big blue eyes, and his fair hair curling like the young tendrils of the vine. I elect to do nothing whatever of the kind. He is simply a very grave problem and study to me; and whither his life-journey may tend I am sure I don't know. For the sake of his few surviving relatives I trust that he will not be hanged; but who knows? Who can tell?

> " Oh toi qui passes par ce cloître,
> Recueilles-toi : tu n'es pas sûr
> De voir s'allonger et s'accroître
> Un autre jour ton ombre au mur."

So sings very sweetly and sadly M. Théophile Gautier. So is it with the most tenderly-nurtured childhood. This little boy, I humbly hope, will lack no careful blue-aproned gardener, no hot-water pipes, no artful composts or well-glazed conservatory to grow him; but when he is grown, what next? Can I insure the fruit against the inroads of innumerable animalculæ, now to us invisible? For the credit of humanity, I hope and believe that most of those who have the

charge of a child regard that charge as awful in
its responsibilities. I look around and see
churches and schools crowded with young children ; but, alas, are they only the neglected or the
ill-treated ones who come to grief? The ab-
surdity of a mother telling you that the baby she
is nursing is to be an engineer or a barrister
seems palpable enough ; but do not the sternest,
most matter-of-fact parents and guardians fall
into absurdities quite as ridiculous? Try to
speculate upon the future of the thousands of
charity children whose silver voices float upwards, once a year, into the dusky space of the
Great Dome of St. Paul's. Essay to predict what
is to become of the eight hundred Eton boys who
are flocking into the Great Western Railway
carriages, and coming whooping home from the
holidays. The charity boys and girls are sedulously and piously taught ; the Eton boys are
watched over by grave and learned divines,
destined perchance to become archbishops. And
what next? "That living flood, pouring through
those streets, of all qualities, all ages, knowest
thou whence it is coming, whither it is going?
Aus der Ewigkeit, zu der Ewigkeit hin—From
Eternity, onwards to Eternity. These are ap-
paritions : what else?"

The philoprogenitive reader will have scarcely
failed to discover long before this that the little

boy I have been speaking of does not belong to
me. Indeed he is no child of mine. Albeit I
am his Uncle, no blood of mine is in his veins.
He is a smiling young Anglo-Saxon, with an
English face and English eyes. This admis
sion may, as I have hinted, be entirely super-
fluous. Lord bless you! if he were my child,
I should have broken out long since, in rap-
tures. I should have apostrophised him as
my pet, my poppet, my darling, my winsome,
tricksome baby-boy. He knows that I regard
him as neither winsome nor tricksome, and that
I would rather not have any of his tricks. There
is nobody in the house to call him poppet or pet,
or to cuddle and cocker him. Until he grows
up and loses his heart to a woman, or has money
to lend to a man, he will find none to flatter him.
"Poor neglected cherub!" the fond mother may
exclaim, "to pine away under this cold, harsh
tutelage!" I don't think, to judge from his ringing laughter, and the quantity of bread and butter he eats, that he is at all disposed to pine
away. Indeed he seems to be about as happy as
the day is long. If, by Heaven's wisdom, he has
been deprived of that flood of passionate affection
which only parents can bestow, he is safe, on the
other hand, from those tempests of unjust anger
and ferocity in which only parents are permitted
to indulge. I have generally found that the in-

dulgent parents thrash their darlings most. The spoilt child gets seldom that most inestimable boon in education—EQUITY—in the judgments passed upon him; that Equity which is " the right witness that considereth all the particular circumstances of the deed, the which also is tempered with the sweetness of mercy." In households where the honey-pot is always open, there seldom fails to be an abundance of wax (spelt " whacks"); yet do I hope to solve the problem of bringing up a child that I have not begotten without spoiling and without laying a finger on him.

O ho! this paragraph must surely awaken Hircius and Spungius. " Misanthrope! Egotist! Vile sciolist!" I hear those worthies yelp. " Miserable Yahoo, following in the trail of Swift. Does he, forsooth, wish to enter the nursery like an ogre, and declare war upon infants? What does he know about children? Had he ever a baby?" Even so, I am childless; but am I out of court? Hircius, I know, has fruitful loins. He has but to cast a stone over the workhouse wall to hit one of his brats. Spungius is great in babies; deafens people with their praises while alive, borrows money to bury them when they die. If I had ever known this little boy in babyhood, I think I could manage to say something sentimental on the baby-question. It would have been egotistical, but still an egotism that the

whole world pardons. This is the country of
baby worship; and the baby-devotee is never
accused of being an idolater. It is a safe thing
to·write sentimentally about babies. Baby literature is sure to sell. Some modern authors have
taken to saying their prayers in print; others to
praising their own works ; and a few to abusing
their species ; but the most popular form of literature is that which lends itself to pouring melted
butter over one's own chicks. Here, by my bedside is a fat little volume, gorgeous in crimson
and gold, lately put out by Messrs. Routledge,
and bearing the highly popular name of
William C. Bennett. I open the book at ran-
dom, and read :

> " Cheeks as soft as July peaches ;
> Lips whose dewy scarlet teaches
> Poppies paleness ; round large eyes,
> Ever great with new surprise.
>   *   *   *   *
> Clutching fingers, straightening jerks,
> Twining feet whose each toe works.
>   *   *   *   *
> Slumbers—such sweet angel seemings,
> That we'd ever have such dreamings.
>   *   *   *   *
> Gladness brimming over gladness ;
> Joy in ease, delight.in sadness ;
> Lovliness beyond completeness ;
> Sweetness distancing all sweetness;
> Beauty all that Beauty may be,—
> That's MAY BENNETT, that's my baby."

There are over two-score couplets in this poem;
but I have only been able to quote a few lines.
I am not at all inclined to sneer at these verses
as namby-pamby, or to cavil at such somewhat
too plastic versification as "gladness" and "sad-
ness," "seemings" and "dreamings." I am
glad to recognise in Mr. William C. Bennett a
very tender, musical, fascinating lyrist. I am
sure he means all that he says, and more. I am
given to understand that he has earned the title
of the "Laureate of the Babies," and that his
chirping, kindly books sell by tens of thousands.
And I shall not have, perhaps, one in a thousand
readers who will regard my view of the baby
question with anything but contempt and abhor-
ence. I turn over the leaves of Mr. Bennett's
pretty book, and light on an infinity of baby
lyrics: "Baby May," "Baby's shoes," "Tod-
dling May," "Cradle songs," "Mother's songs,"
"To our Baby Kate," "Epitaphs for infants,"
"On a Dead Infant," and many more on the
same sweet, well-worn, but not worn-out theme.
I have already expressed my faith in Mr. Bennett's sincerity. In his engraved portrait by the
frontispiece he looks like a man who loves
babies; and thousands of mothers, I have no
doubt, tearfully murmured "God bless him!"
when they read his poems. Surely it is wicked,
sardonic, to come prowling into this baby para-

dise and trample down the daisies. But Duty is
a stern monitor, and Duty compels me to ask
whether the intensity of baby worship *does not
depend, after all, on circumstances, and whether
those circumstances do not often alter cases in a
very strange and melancholy manner ?* It is
probable that Mr. Bennett lives in a very nice
house, and has everything that heart can wish
for ; that his babies are brought to him at proper
times and seasons, duly spruced and 'beautified,
and that there is a five-barred gate on the nursery landing to prevent his young ones tumbling
down-stairs. Viewed through this radiant medium, this atmosphere of blue-kid shoes and
satin bows, pap-spoons, corals, laced robes, embroidered hoods, and plumed hats—with any
amount of baby linen procurable from the Spon-
salia, and a kind doctor always ready round the
corner in case of infantile ailments—the baby
becomes indeed a delight and a treasure ; it is
another element in British comfort. It is as
much a part of papa's home joys as his slippers,
his " Illustrated News," or his evening tumbler.
A well-to-do middle-class house is hardly complete without a filter, a Kent's knife-cleaner, a
moderator lamp, and a baby. All these articles
are to be found in their several places, and minister in their several degrees to the felicity and
solace of those who possess them. But how

about the hovel where a baby is born, and there
is nothing but a baker's old jacket to wrap it
in? How about the babies of shame that are
packed up in hampers, strangled in secret places,
flung into dustbins, deserted on doorsteps? Who
writes sonnets on the workhouse babies, or
mourns over their fate when they are burnt to
death by twenties? When poverty and nakedness and hunger sit grinning on the poor man's
hearth, is the sick baby a household joy or a
household misery? Oh, my brethren (since
homilies are the fashion), how we brag and
boast and bemuse ourselves about our own
babies, and how little we reck about what becomes of other people's babies! How the pious
and decorous matron drives from her door the
wretched nursemaid who has a base-born infant!
If this baby worship were sincere, and not a
congested kind of personal vanity, often grotesque enough, and of which the still more ludi-
crous side was to be seen in the abominable
American baby-shows, should we not feel inclined to devise some measures to prevent babies
being murdered or starved, to force profligate
men to make provision for their by-blows?
What is the much-vaunted baby in the manufacturing districts but a thing to be drugged with
"cordials" and "elixirs," or to be "overlaid?"
Ask the parish undertaker what he knows about

the dark side of babyhood. Ask the parish
doctor, ask Dr. Lankester the coroner. We go
on simpering forth fiddledee about our own
babies, and pass, indifferent, through a whole
Golgotha of dead babies' bones. I am as poor,
Heaven knows, as Job, and have a hard struggle
to make both ends meet; yet I would cheerfully
work my fingers to the bone, and be my hundred pounds to any one else's hundred, to estab-
lish were it the tiniest nucleus of a *real* FOUND-
LING HOSPITAL in lieu of that sham place in
Guildford Street, where the "mother" is to
"present herself before the committee" before
the foundling can be admitted. I declare that
jobbed and perverted charity is enough to
make the bones of THOMAS CORAM turn in their
grave.

When I read of the delightful, smiling, tod-
dling little thing Mr. Bennett so charmingly de-
scribes—when I see the baby portraits and
baby "pistolgrams" advertised—when I wander
in a wilderness of perambulators, india-rubber
balls, lollipops, hoops, kid-shoes, and so forth
—I think sometimes that it is good to hang
a bunch of hyssop in the wine cup, and to ask
whether we do not plume ourselves somewhat
too much about the beauty and happiness and
purity of babyhood. I think I have glanced
more than once upon a poor little gasping lump

of damp dough with a chronic stomach-ache. I think Shakespeare has drawn in half a dozen words a terrible life-like picture of the human baby. And, as a final corrective to overweening pride in babies, I turn to my Thomas à Kempis, and in the preface read these true and mournful . lines:

"*The human infant is a picture of such deformity, weakness, nakedness, and helpless distress, as is not to be found among the home-born animals of this world. The chicken has its birth from no sin, and therefore comes forth in beauty; it runs and pecks as soon as its shell is broken; the calf and the lamb go both to play as soon as the dam is delivered of them; they are pleased with themselves, and please the eye that beholds their frolicksome state and beauteous clothing; whilst the new-born babe of a woman, that is to have an upright form, and view the heavens, and worship the God that made them, lies for months in gross ignorance, weakness and impurity; as sad a spectacle when he first breathes the life of this world, as when, in the agonies of death, he breathes his last.*"

I think it would do all of us good, the childful as well as the childless, to ponder a little over these words before we bragged too much about Baby.

ON MR. MAVOR'S SPELLING-BOOK.

My Library is not a very extensive one. The publishers rarely send me copies of new works, for the very sufficient reason that, when they do, I generally abuse them. My brother authors, I fear, don't like me, and I certainly don't like *them;* and so they have given up forwarding me presentation copies of their productions. On my few shelves, I am glad to say, there are no works of my own.

Who would wish to preserve the double-tooth, wrenched, after so many dire dental struggles, from the unwilling jaw? Who, but a hypochondriac would keep an assorted collection of coffin nails in his study—and what are a man's own printed writings but so many nails in his coffin? When one has been long on the rack, and is quit of it till to-morrow morning, it is as well to double-lock the door of the Torture-Room, and hide the dismal engine of agony from view.

How you, my eminent friend, regard the little novels, essays, dramas, poems, etc., your facile pen has composed, I know not. To me the labors of my hand are but so many memorials of research in vain, want, anguish, and defeat. But then, perhaps, you are not in the habit of wrestling with wild-beasts at Ephesus, or of endeavoring to convince a perverse generation. Better, no doubt, to be a comfortable lion in the Ephesian managerie, and to take one's shinbone of beef thankfully. In the preface to his noblest work, says Father Paul: " *Tengo per fermo che quest' opera sarà di pochi letta, ed in breve tempo mancherà di vita, non tanto per diffetto di forma, quanto per la natura della materia,*"—which in our tongue signifieth this: that there is no use in striving; that if your book has all the learning of Bellarmin, and all the acumen of Dom Calmet, and all the painstaking of Florez, and all the majesty of Tillotson, and all the eloquence of Taylor, and all the wit of Swift, it shall not save its author from being sneered at, in a bankrupt review, as an ignorant dolt—sneered at by a boy-critic, who six months since was caned at school ; that, cunning, artistically, as your book may be, it must be essentially fading and ephemeral; and that the highest tide of success will not rescue it at last from the fourpenny-box at a bookstall.

And woe to him, unless he be a Giant, who dedicates his work to Posterity, and trusts in after ages to do him justice. Posterity ! Posterity

will singe a goose with your *magnum opus*.
After ages! They will wrap penn'orths of pud-
ding in the unsold sheets of your Epic. Waters
of Marah to him who deems himself a benefactor
to his kind, and holds himself as necessary to the
world's scheme! Jeremy Bentham so did; and
who, save a few who meet once a year to dine
with his mummy, are grateful to Jeremy Bentham, the Father of Reform? Necessary! "It is
the disease of Princes," said Napoleon (when he
found that the nations had had enough of him),
"to believe themselves necessary. No man is
necessary—I, no more than the others. Alexander and Cæsar are dead, and still the world
rolls on its course without them." And let this
be a warning to you, Tupper, hero of six-and-forty
editions.

And yet I know there are authors who love to
look upon the things they have written—nay,
dote upon them, calling them by endearing
names, thinking the worst the best, and bestowing Grollier and Renaissance bindings, gold
scrolling, and blind tooling upon them. Our
deformed brats are often the best beloved. So
used Monsieur François-Marie-Arouet, called Voltaire, to fondle his multifarious writings. Behold the weazened, shrivelled, hatchet-faced,
wicked-eyed Patriarch of Ferney, in coat of cut-
velvet, and silken-covered spindle-shanks, and

towering white periwig, hugging the *Edito Princeps* of his "Pucelle," which he has had bound in sable morocco. When he is in a good temper, he caresses the scurril tome, and calls it "*Ma Jeanne—ma Jeanneton !*"—the old rascal! When he is in evil case, and bethinks himself that a Day must come for frying and howling, he spurns the polecat thing, and cries "*Ce livre-là a été écrit par un laquais ivre.*" The great authors of the present day may be equally partial to their bantlings.

And those great authors, who are they? Let me hasten to name the Editor of "Zadkiel's Almanac," the scholar and gentleman who pens the dramatic criticisms in the "London Gazette" (published by authority), and Mr. George Francis Train. I would have whispered thy name, my Hircius; but thou art modest. Spungius, thy alias should have been added to the list, but that I know thee to be fierce in opposition to the present Ministry; nor would I expose Lord Palmerston by indiscreetly calling attention to thy merits to the humiliation of seeing a proffered pension refused by Spungius, the upright and incorruptible.

"*Ah, que nous ne sommes rien !*" cried Bossuet, preaching on earthly vanities before the gilded court at Versailles, who, of a certainty, thought "some punkins" of themselves. Oh,

Eagle of Meaux, thou errest! Evil is an entity, and we are bad; and to be bad is to be something. For instance, this morning, Breakfasting in Bed, I feel as bad as bad can be, morally and physically. It is an abominable foggy morning. I have complained of the fog, which is wrong. To be right I should have been resigned to any little variation in the weather. Then I was angry because they would not let me have any muffins.

Why should I be deprived of muffins? There used to be muffins. But four months since, I had new-laid eggs every morning at dear old U. C.; I never thought of Breakfasting in Bed there. Now, a dingy bolus, with dusky specks of straw glued to its shell, reminds me, by its mustiness, of the blessings of the Anglo-French Treaty of Commerce. A French egg this, and charged at the price of a new-laid one. The newspapers, too, came late. The mendacious newsboy said that the "machine had broken down." What! all the machines? Was there, then, a conspiracy against all the presses in pressdom? In fact, it was this lack of journalism that led me first to quarrel with my breakfast, and then to begin thinking about books, and thence to turn to their writers, and then to bemoan myself, and say that I didn't like my brother authors; whereas, the truth is, that I love them dearly, every one. Bless them! It is clear that I am in an envious, discontented, and thoroughly uncharitable state of mind this morning.

Will the little book I keep under my pillow console me? I turn up page 167, and read, " Constantly endeavor to do the will of another rather than thy own. Constantly prefer a state of want to a state of abundance. Constantly choose the lowest place, and to be inferior to all. He that doeth this, enters into the regions of rest and peace." These beautiful words either mean something or nothing. They cannot be accepted with a Jesuitical reservation. If I construe them literally, I must, if my publishers tell me to write down freedom, progress, and education, do their will and not my own, which runs in precisely the contrary direction. I must abandon all hopes of muffins, because it is the will of others that I should not have them. I must constantly prefer going in rags, dwelling in a garret, and pinching my belly, to wearing warm broadcloth, to living in a snug house, to dining on roast mutton. If I am invited to take the chair at the annual festival of the Charitable Crumpet-Makers, I must decline the honor, or solicit employment as a waiter or plate-washer at the London Tavern. The sentences I have quoted are not from an inspired writer, and I am therefore guiltless of irreverence in discussing

them; but I saw lately in the shop-window of a
stationer in Chancery Lane a schedule of rules to
be observed by pious persons in the conduct of
their daily life, each rule fortified by a scriptural
text.

I say boldly, that if we acted up to the letter
of these rules, society could not exist, and the
world would become a howling desert. How
could we get on if nobody took the chair; if
everybody went tattered, and denied himself
food; if nobody exerted the Will that Heaven
has implanted in him? And is it not the grossest
simulation, the most "unsophisticated hypocrisy,"
as Sir Jonah Barrington pleonastically puts it, to
go on chattering about what we ought to do,
when we are perfectly aware that we cannot do
it, and that the whole scheme of human government and society forbids us even to attempt it?

Whereupon I return to my Library. The
motive of my alluding to it at all you shall presently hear. I am cudgelling my brains to remember if it contains a Spelling-book. It is *so*
many years since I conned that useful volume.
Dictionaries and vocabularies I have galore, in
many tongues. Do I not prize a certain dimly-
printed collection of "Domestic Dialogues,"
written in French, German, Russian, and Latin,
in which there is positively a conversation on
drinking beer and smoking tobacco: "*De Fic-*

tilibus tubis ad usum Nicotiana." Says A of
the Virginian weed : "*Equidem fumi haustu
non utor, sed pulvere abutor.*" A is no smoker,
but a snuffer. Remarks the Ciceronian B of
beer, "*Cerevisia inter Nicotiana usum gratior
gustus, sine quâ ne uti quidem hac possum ;
quippe qui sitim creet.*" This classical gentleman.
thinks that a glass of Allsopp's Bitter goes well
with a pipe of bird's-eye, and acknowledges himself a beery one; for tobacco parches a man,
says he. Then have I not the learned Harris's
"Hermes", of which more anon, as the profound
Hodderius says ; and Sir John Stoddart's "Universal Grammar," which to me is as universal
confusion as Kant's "Critique of Pure Reason,"
(which Spungius understands so well) ? I pass
over Trench "On Words," Grose's "Lexicon Bala-
tronicum," Pegge's "Defence of the Cockney Dialect," and Horne Tooke's "Diversions of Purley ;"
for this morning I thirst only for a Spelling-book.
Where is Mavor ? Is there a Mavor in the
House ? The newspapers arrive, and I become
more and more anxious for a Spelling-book.

There is, it would seem, no work of reference
of that description in my Library; but at last a
dog's-eared fasciculus, much blurred with pencil-
marks, and smutched and smirched—I trust not
with infant tears—is discovered in the possession
of the Little Boy introduced to the reader in the

second of these Papers. He is at first loth to
give up Mavor; but he at least is practically
taught that it is his duty to do another's will in
preference to his own. Mavor is taken from him
for the use of his cruel uncle; but a written re-
ceipt and explanation of cause for detention is
given to him, to bear him harmless on his arrival
at Miss Mangnall's establishment.

Here is Mavor at last. Revised by Cecil Hart-
ley, A.M.; the one hundred and seventieth thousand. Here are the famous short lessons: "His
pen has no ink in it;" "I met a man with a pig;"
"Do as you are told, or it may be bad for you."
This is rather fierce in its minatory style, and
Dr. Mavor must have got it from Dr. Busby.
"Come, James, make haste. Now read your
book. Here is a pin to point with." ' Little boys
are not allowed to point with pins nowadays.
"Tom fell in the pond. He was a bad boy. Jack
Hall was a good boy. He took pains to learn as
he ought, and made all the great boys his friends."
But these characters have been, I think, more
tersely sketched in the unpublished Nursery Edda
of the Titmarshian Sage:

> "Little Jack Snook,
> Was fond of his book,
> And was much beloved by his master;
> *But naughty Jack Spry*
> *Has got a black eye,*
> *And carries his nose in a plaster.*"

Then comes the story of the nice girl, but who was not good, and told fibs, and whose cake was eaten by a mouse; then the apologue of Miss Jane Bond, who had a new doll, aud whose good aunt gave her some cloth *to make a shift for it.* O Mr. Cecil Hartley, A.M., do you call this editing Mavor? You should have discreetly substituted for that sad passage about the S— a neat paragraph to the effect that Miss Jane Bond's aunt proceeded to the Lilliputian Warehouse in Regent Street, and there purchased some " underclothing " for her niece's doll.

This benevolent lady was doubtless the Mrs. Bond who appears to have kept an inn or hotel in the rural districts, and who, when the travellers were hungry and desired that their stomachs might be filled, cried out to the ducks in the pond, "Dilly, dilly, dilly, come and be killed;" but they would not, whereupon Mrs. Bond

> "Flew in a very great rage,
> With plenty of onions and plenty of sage."

And it was bad for the ducks, because they would not do what they were told.

Frank Pitt and his fat cheeks; Jane whose hand was tied up in a cloth; the girl who tied the string to the bird's leg; and Harry who gorged his cake and was sick; and Peter Careful, who ate a little piece of his cake (the young curmudgeon!) every day, but kept it till it grew mouldy and worthless: all these friends of my youth I meet and pass by; and then I come to Richard—Richard Cœur de Lion he ought to be called—who said to his schoolmates, " I have got a cake; let us go and eat it ;" and when they had all eaten, there remained a piece, which Richard put by, saying, "I will eat it to-morrow." But a blind man came into the play-ground— but Mavor shall tell the rest : "He said, 'My pretty lads, if you will, I will play you a tune.' and they all left their sport, and came and stood round him. And Richard saw that while he played, the tears ran down his cheeks. And Richard said, ' Old man, why do you cry ?' And the old man said, ' Because I am hungry : I have no-bo-dy to give me any dinner or supper : I have nothing in the world but this little dog, and I cannot work. If I could work I would.' Then Richard went, without saying a word, and fetched the rest of his cake, which he had intended to eat another day; and he said, ' Here, old man, here is some cake for you.' The old man said, ' Where is it? for I am blind; I cannot see it.' So Richard put it into his hat. And the fiddler thanked him ; and Richard was more glad than if he had eaten ten cakes himself."

I wish that Mr. Mulready or Mr. Webster would take Richard and the blind fiddler as a subject for a picture; and I have often thought this simple story to be one of the noblest and most pathetic narratives in the English language.

. Still turning over the trim tome. bound in green cloth, which, by virtue of a forced loan . from the Little Boy, has come into my possession, I cannot avoid murmuring that it is not the Mavor of my youth; that it has experienced change, and that the change has not been one for the better. My old spelling-book was bound in light-speckled sheepskin, and had a warm, portmanteau-like odor. The modern Mavor has portraits of animals, drawn with symmetry and vigor by Mr. Harrison Weir; the old book was decorated with the vilest vignettes that sign-painter turned draughtsman ever imagined, or wood-chopper flourishing long before Bewick or Thurston ever hacked. Strange heraldic-looking animals—griffins, unicorns, roaring bulls of Bashan, monsters and chimeras dire—passed current for lions and tigers and the domestic animals. But what did we little children care, so long as we could smear the coarse cartoons with blue and red and yellow ochre? And was the fable of the Dog and the Shadow less suggestive because the dog was not in the least like his adumbrated duplicate, and was besides as big, according to the scale of comparison, as the elephant in the next cut? And the frontispiece, again!

The new Mavor shows a pretty tableaux of

Home; a young mother, surrounded by a chirping little brood of those children whom Mr. Gilbert draws so charmingly—little girls in long curls and short trousers, cherub-faced boys in pretty tunics. They are hanging over the spelling-book with as much pleased interest in their little faces as though Mavor were Baron Munchausen. In the foreground is a toy-horse of the regular buff-coat and red-wafer pattern. Ah, dear me, dear me! the old Mavor had a very different kind of frontispiece. Showed it not three grim compartments, stages or floors; in the uppermost a boy-class of shivering little wretches, ranged before the desk of a stern usher, who wore his hat and bore a cane?

We all settled that this was an usher; for although ferocious, he looked poor. There was a frigid gloom about that top-storey picture, at once suggestive of the horrible winter mornings at school, the lessons before breakfast, and agonizing incandescence produced in numbed palms by "spats" of the cane. The middle compartment represented a ladies'-school: *such* a Miss Tickletoby in the chair, *such* a Mrs. Teachem!

> "Come here, Master Timothy Todd—
>   Before we have done you'll look grimmer;
> You've been spelling some time for the rod,
>   But I'll have you to know I'm a Trimmer."

I am sure Thomas Hood must have had the woodcut portrait of this terrible old dame in his mind's eye when he wrote (and illustrated) the fancy portrait of Mrs. Trimmer in his "Comic Annual."

It may be that I have been mixing up the pictures of the old Mavor with those of the old Dilworth. At all events, both spelling-books had strange representations of boys in frills, and coats with two-inch tails, of schoolmistresses in mob-caps, and pedagogues in long dressing-gowns. And Dilworth and Mavor were both illustrated with "cuts," while intempestive contemplation of their wood-blocks brought little boys into intimate connection with another block of wood, whence the engravings are struck off in red ink. I do not wish any one to laugh at these forced jests. Let them shudder, and shut up Mavor.

But why did I ever open him? What have I to do at my age with a baby's spelling-book? A great deal, I think. Mavor is an admirable corrective for conceit. A cursory reference to his pages will tell many a scholar, inflated with the big books he has been studying, a great many things he did not know before. I declare that, until breakfast time this morning, I did not know—or had forgotten—that cow's-horn is "used instead of glass for lanterns." I had

heard, of course, of horn lanterns, but deemed
them to be obsolete. Judge of my astonishment to find them glimmering in the Mavor of
1862 !

Again, that the white hair of goats was "valu-
able for wigs." Ignoramus ! I thought that bar-
risters' wigs were made of horsehair, and the
Lord Mayor's coachman's jasey of spun-glass.
We are never too old to learn.

The which confirms me in my estimate of the
advantage we may derive from occasionally consulting in mature life the simplest elementary
works. What do we know about things, after
all ? I should like to get this exceedingly wide-
awake Bishop Colenso into a corner, and put
him through a course of Mavor, and Pinnock,
and Mangnall, and the " Guide to Knowledge."
The right reverend father is the author of a very
good book on arithmetic, I am told; but I doubt
whether he has been lately bestowing much
attention on such simple problems as " If a her-
ring and a half cost three-halfpence, how many
herrings can you get for a shilling ?" Propound
this to me, O Colenso ! Do you know what ink
is made of ? Can you tell me how the angles of
Westminster Abbey are subtended on the retina
of a bull's-eye ? Do you know anything about
the manufacture of boot-varnish ? Can you
bite-in a copper-plate ? Do you know who in-

vented braces ?   Can you inform me when steel
pens were first used ?   Can you find me a rhyme
for Hippopotamus ?   Could you undertake to
supply a weekly satirico-political cartoon for
" Punch ?"   Can you define what human wit is ?
Do you know (but here I borrow from sturdy old
PALEY) how oval frames are turned ?

Go away Bishop of the Black Man !   Go
to your Pinnock, or to your " Punch " even ; for
you would derive more wisdom from the study
of that periodical, than from puzzling your
poor brains about the Pentateuch !   Before the
doubts of a Hume, a Gibbon, a Volney, a Voltaire, a Condorcet, a Mirabeau, one stands
amazed, aghast, to see the mighty intellects ob-
scured by clouds, the giants ridden by the incu-
bus who wears a cock's feather in his cap, and
in a shrill fluted voice Denies, Denies for ever.
Before the perplexities of a Pascal, a Hobbes, a
Gassendi, one stands awed and hushed.   Nay,
in the reckless foaming infidel, his hands
clenched, his eyes glaring, his hair blown about
by the Eternal Storm, and vociferating his
hoarse " No !" there is something gigantic,
though appalling.   There may be abandonment,
but there may be rectitude.   The martyrs of
unbelief are often as self-sacrificing as the martyrs of faith.   But for this small-beer scepticism,
this Tom Paineism in a white choker, this

Straussology adapted to small tea-parties, this genteel free-thinking for family reading—faugh! it tastes in the mouth like a bad groat.

Off, Dr. C.! Away, Mr. Wilkie Collinso! I will have none of your "sensations" about the Books of Moses. And, butler—my butler wears crinoline—H. M. and B. J. are coming to dinner to-day, and we will have a bottle of the right red seal, not the cheap Cape I have bought lest Spungius should pop in. For I love not South-African port—nay, nor South-African theology.

And before I shut up my Mavor, there is a particular class in society to which I desire to commend the attentive study of the Spelling-book. O you noble captains, you brave swells, you honest, jovial, intrepid, kind-hearted, ignorant young officers in the Heavies and in the Prancers, rush off to your booksellers and invest in all the copies of the spelling-books that remain unsold. Let your devotion henceforth be to Mars, Bacchus, and Apollo—but don't forget Mavor. If more English gentlemen belonging to the military patrician class, had a commonly decent acquaintance with English orthography, don't you think that we should have fewer "bubble bets," that the Admiral would not " abhor" the Colonel quite so often, and that one's Breakfast in Bed would not be poisoned by the "Turf scandals," of which the recapitulation has been lately the nuisance and disgrace of the morning newspapers?

Don't think that I wish to launch into a violent tirade against Colonel Rawdon Crawley, or Captain De Boots, or Lieutenant Guy Livingstone. I think them much better fellows than Colonel James, or Captain Booth, or Lieutenant Lismahago. Nay, when I compare them with M. le Chef le Bataillon Fracasse de la Tapagerie, or M. le Capitaine Gamelle Boutenfeu, I strike the balance in favor of the English officer, and think him no worse soldier for being a gentleman. But he should learn to spell. He should, indeed. Colonel Rawdon Crawley should be able ·to write his letters without the aid of a "Johnson's Dictionary;" Captain De Boots should be cured of spelling kept "kep," and Mediterranean "Meddytirainian."

I know that Lord Malmesbury doesn't attach much value to accurate orthography; and I can guess the reason. His Lordship's father was that same learned Mr. Harris who wrote the "Hermes"—alluded to at the commencement of this Paper—and who was one of the most erudite philological writers of whom this country can boast. Depend upon it, that the noble Lord had quite enough spelling-book cheer in his youth to last him for a lifetime; the pastrycook's boy

doesn't care much for jam-tarts ; the tailor's son
is reluctant to assume the shears and French
chalk of Mr. Snip, his papa, deceased.   But Mavor is not to be banished from polite society because Malmesbury frowns.

I hope that, ere very long, at least a dozen
Spelling-books may be added to the libraries of
the Senior and Junior United Service, the
Guards, and the Army and Navy Clubs. They
need not entirely supersede the study of the
" Racing Calendar," or " Ruff's Guide to the
Turf ;" but they may be instrumental in spreading a mild and innocent love for the contemplation of words in two syllables, and eventually
cause " Turf scandals "—if the Turf *must* be
scandalous ; a quality I do not hold to be 'at all
necessary to a noble and manly national pursuit—to turn on some other topic than the orthography of Reindeer as against Raindeer.

ON THE PREVAILING MADNESS.

FROM all that I can see, or hear, or am told, and from a little, perhaps, that I feel, I am inclined to apprehend that there is a good deal of Madness going about the world just now. If Sir Baldwin Leighton's Night Poaching Act is definitively to put down the unlicensed capture of feathered and furry game (which it will no more do than it will enable me to marry my grandmother), it should surely have contained a clause to warrant the shutting up, under the certificate of two physicians, of all the hares next March ; for if they catch the epidemic which is raging among humanity, the chances are that they will go very mad indeed. This is most decidedly a mad world, my masters. Don't you think the Americans have gone mad, and that "a dark house and a whip" would be the fittest treatment for the delirium which has driven a mighty nation into the perpetration of political bankruptcy ? They *must* be mad, only they have duplicity enough not to howl or tear their flesh, or scrabble at the gate (as King David did when he *feigned* madness), until they have withdrawn

themselves from public observation. In one of
Mr. Dickens's earlier works there is a terrific tale
of a lunatic, who so kept the secret of his insanity for very many years. He slew his wife,
and raved finely to himself when alone; but as
he wore a white neckcloth, talked about the weather, and lent money at interest in polite society,
he was accounted perfectly sane; until, as ill
luck would have it, it occurred to him to brain
his brother-in-law with a chair, and to avow, in
a succession of short yelps, that he was raving
mad; whereupon his relatives had out a commission *De Lunatico* against him, and locked him
up, incontinent. It is a dangerous matter to
meddle with your brother-in-law. As a rule,
your father-in-law is merely a harmless bore, who
borrows money from you, and in quiet confidence imparts to his friends the opinion that you
never were quite the sort of fellow for his Emily;
but your *beau-frère has got his mother's blood
in him;* and the children of the horseleech are
younger and stronger than their parent. I knew
a man of rare talent once, who went out of his
mind; whereupon quoth a cynical friend of his:
"What a confounded fool X—— must be! It's
just like his indiscretion to go blurting out what
nobody wanted to know. *I've been madder than
he for years;* but I always took good care not to
let anybody know it." How would it be if some

sapient physician suddenly discovered that all those exterminating patriots in America yonder were mad,—that "Uncle Abe" had only ninety-nine cents out of the mental dollar; that there was a tile off Mr. Seward; that Mr. Chase was a gone 'coon? The New Orleans Davoust-Haynau, Butler, may have been suffering, throughout, from cerebral congestion; and the wretch M'Neil, at the time of the Palmyra massacres, was, perchance, quite an unaccountable being. You know the gist of Dr. Forbes Winslow's teaching. The people at home, who govern me by making me think that I govern them, have carefully put away Dr. W's. big book; which, if a man be at all nervous, he is apt to consult as frequently as though it were a kind of psychical looking-glass. A stumble or a stutter, inability to chip your egg in the proper manner, over drowsiness or over wide-awakedness, dimness of sight, or swimming in the head, or carillons in the ears, may all be so many symptoms of morbid diseases of the brain and mind. If you feel any one of these symptoms, the best thing you can do is to buy a strait-waistcoat, and go off at once to Dr. Forbes Winslow, lest worse should ensue. This is the key-stone of the Winslowian philosophy.

But what would the learned Doctor think of the cerebral condition of the Distracted States? Is Dixié's Land a whit saner than Columbia?

One of my newspapers this morning tells me that the dark gentleman who had formerly the honor of driving the President of Secessia's carriage is just now in England, and is lecturing about among the pious folks with as profitable results to himself, I hope, as those hinted at by Mr. George Borrow in his "Wild Wales." What says Jefferson Davis's quondam slave of his master? Is the Confederate Dictator a hero to his body-coachman? The ex-Jehu declares that Jeff. "isn't of much account." When things go smoothly, he is pleasant and placable enough; but when their course is roughened, he storms and goes on the rampage in the "skeariest" manner. I dare say that he is as mad as all the rest of the world.

When his Lordship of Dundreary is unable to discern the drift of a particular observation, he forthwith puts down the speaker as a lunatic. Why should not his Lordship be right—or any other "fellah?" I dare say that Mr. Sothern (if he condescended to read the first number of "Breakfast in Bed") thought me as mad as a hatter for presuming to question the perfection of his impersonation. For my part, I have a firm persuasion of the lunacy of the people who grow ecstatic about Dundreary, or who sip their grog while the great Olmar, or the greater Léotard, or the greatest Blondin may be capering over their heads, at the imminent risk of tumbling down and smashing the skulls both of spectators and acrobats. I think that to take Drury Lane Theatre—if you have any money to lose—is a sign of mental alienation so decided, that the mere act of signing the agreement should be a full warrant for the friends of the manager taking care of him. I think half the people who are quaking with terror through fear of garotters, and cutting their trembling fingers with the bowie-knives they don't know how to handle—I speak with authority in this matter, for I have been garotted, and it didn't hurt me—are mad.

I am sure the garotters are mad; poor, purblind, darkened, demented creatures, running their heads against Newgate granite walls as a bull runs at a gate. I don't think that Sir Joshua Jebb is quite right in his mind when he countersigns a ticket-of-leave; and I have little doubt but that if a commission sat upon Sir Walter Crofton, they would discover that he was subject to delusions. The question is, I take it, less to find out who is mad than who isn't mad. Do you mean to tell me there is not a screw loose in the brainpan of those Greeks who are persisting in electing the candidate who won't stand, and in carting about, on the top of an omnibus, as though it were the Golden Calf or an image of Juggernaut, the portrait of a Young

4

Middy of whom they know nothing? And that fine old Tory, the King of Prussia!

When the drill-sergeant monarch makes a speech to a loyal deputation from Kalbsfleisch-stein on the necessity of governing " outside the constitution," don't you think him as crazy as his ancestor who used to cane his son Fritz and throw plates and dishes at his daughter Wilhel-mina ; or as his brother deceased, who was wont to wash his poor wandering head in Vermicelli soup? And the illustrious historian of the Ho-henzollerns! Is all quite right at Chelsea, think you, when Great Tom booms forth peals of praise over tyranny and brutality, and makes a demi-god of the beery and brutal old bludgeon-man and crockery-breaker, with his Tabaks-Collegium, and other tomfooleries?

When Lady Caroline Lamb (herself as de-mented as Madge Wildfire) first met Lord Byron, she made this entry against his name in her diary : " Mad, bad, and dangerous to know." Lady Morgan, who tells the story, and whose bald and frivolous tittle-tattle has just been pub-lished under the auspices of Mr. Hepworth Dixon as an " Autobiography "—shade of " P.P., clerk of this parish," has it come to this ?—was mad with vanity and Radical politics.

A mad generation will eagerly read all the antiquated gossip and scanmag of Dublin Castle

during the mad viceroyalty of the Duke of
Richmond (who is said to have knighted a link-
man between claret and coffee one night), and
will chuckle over the eccentricities of the epoch
when the ladies of the Irish Court—titled ladies
—used to play at the pastoral game of " Cutcha-
kachoo," which consisted in squatting down on
the carpet with your hands clasped underneath
your hams, and changing places with your
partner as rapidly as was possible in that abnormal position. And Prince Puckler Muskau,
whom Lady Morgan's friends used to call Prince
Pickle Mustard, and who, being desirous of
attending a banquet of the " Friends of Freedom," wanted to know if the health of his High
Dutchship would be proposed, and if his right
to precedence as an " Altezza," or Highness,
would be recognized—what are we to think of
him ? The Friends of Freedom didn't want the
" Altezza " at their dinner under any circumstances, and Sir Charles Morgan told him so ;
whereupon my lady fell into an agony of alarm
lest the Prince should insist on fighting a duel
with her husband.

All the people in Lady Morgan's book (which
will be forgotton the day after to-morrow) seem
to be more or less bereft of their senses—from
good-natured old Lady Cork, who used to pilfer
small articles from the shop-counters where she

dealt—of whom I have read, but not in this
" Autobiography "—to John Kemble the tra-
gedian, who once meeting the " wild Irish girl,"
(afterwards Sidney Lady Morgan) at an evening-
party, twined his fingers in her curly black
locks, and said, in a voice husky with port-wine:
" Little girl, where did you get your wig from ?"
Stay, there is one personage in the " Autobiography " who really seems to have possessed
some sense. He was a poet, and bored the
authoress of " The Book of the Boudoir " to get
some of his effusions published; and on her
civilly declining to do so, wrote a second letter
back, to say that he was also a practical boot
and shoe maker, and that he would be very
grateful to my Lady if she would use her influence with Sir Charles Morgan to get him an
order for a pair of boots.

" St. Hierom," says Burton, " out of a strong
imagination, conceived within himself that he
then saw them dancing in Rome; and if thou
shalt either conceive or climb up to see, thou
shalt soon perceive that all the world is mad ;
that it is melancholy, dozes; that it is (which
Epichthonius Cosmopolites expressed not many
years since in a map) made like a fool's head
(with that motto, *Caput helleboro dignum*), a
crazed head; *cavea stultorum*, a fool's para-
dise; or, as Apollonius, a common prison of

gulls, cheaters, flatterers, etc., and needs to be reformed." This is a nice perspective. "For who, indeed," pursues this agreeable moralist, "is not a fool, melancholy, mad? Who is not brain-sick? Folly, Melancholy, Madness, are but one disease." Indeed! "Delirium is a common name to all. Alexander, Gordonius, Jason, Pratensis, Guianerius, Montaltus (*Connaissez-vous ces gens-là ?*), confound them as differing *magis et minus;* so doth David (Psalm xxvii. 5); and 'twas an old Stoical paradox, *omnes stultos insanire*—all fools are mad, though some madder than others. Who is not a fool, or free from Melancholia?" Answer, O Hypochondriac, Breakfast in Bed! "Who is not touched more or less in habit or disposition? What is sickness, as Gregory Tholosanus defines it" (I wish he lived in Saville Row, and would give me an audience between 10 and 1 A.M.), "but a dissolution or perturbation of the bodily league which health combines?" As for the philosophers, they are all, according to the anatomist, as mad as the illiterate. Lactantius, in his Book of Wisdom (can I get it at Mudie's ?), proves them to be dizzards, fools, and madmen, so full of absurd and ridiculous tenets and brain-sick positions (in their critiques on the Pentateuch and elsewhere), that to his thinking, never **any old woman or sick person doted worse.**

Democritus took all from Leucippus, and left, saith he, the inheritance of his folly to Epicurus; which, all spiteful as it was, was never so mad a bequest as that of old Mr. Hartley of Southampton, who left a hundred thousand pounds to build a house for a collection of air-pumps and old bones; and out of which bequest the lawyers have carefully clutched forty thousand pounds for costs of litigation. Plato, Aristippus, and the rest were (according to Lactantius) all idiots; and there was no difference between them and beasts, save that they could speak. Theodoret evinces the same of Socrates. Aristophanes calls him ambitious; his master, Aristotle, *scurra atticus;* Zeno, an enemy to all arts and sciences; Athenius, an opinionative ass, a cavalier, and pedant; Theod. Cyrensis, an atheist and pot-companion, and a very madman in his actions. Bravo, Lactantius! But, dear me, haven't I been aware of Lactantius in modern London? Surely he must be the man who edits the "Cads' Chronicle."

If you desire to hear more about Apollonius, a great wise man, and Julian the Apostate's model author, I refer you to the learned tract of Eusebius against Hierocles. *I* never read it, but Hircius knows it by heart. You will find therein that the actions of the philosophers were prodigious, absurd, ridiculous, and their books and elaborate treatises full of dotage; that their lives were opposite to their words; that they commended poverty in others, and were most greedy and covetous themselves; that they extolled love and peace, and yet persecuted one another with virulent hate and malice. But enough of this *histoire de tout le monde.* If I continue, it will be thought that I am attempting an essay on the History of Civilization.

It is by this time, I hope, satisfactorily settled that you, I, and the majority of mankind are cracked. A famous physician has not hesitated to propound such a theory in a public court of justice; and are we, poor ignorant laymen, to set ourselves against the Royal College of Pall Mall East? Were we not all edified the other day when the poor, meek, placable, ill-used, long-suffering wife of a desperate crockery-dealer in Tottenham Court Road—a " dangerous lunatic," whose horrible hallucinations, springing from " drink and gay company," ending in his daring to protest against the unhappy, persecuted creature, who had been his wedded (and outraged) wife for eight-and-twenty years, indulging in such harmless eccentricities as running up scores with tallymen, pawning his pots and pans, bringing crowds round his shop, and heaping mountains of Billingsgate on his head—were we not all profoundly struck with the perspicuity of the

Law of Lunacy, and the ample guarantees afforded
by the Constitution for the liberty of the subject,
when poor Mrs. Crockery got, by a process as
easy as lying, a medical certificate, empowering
her to lock up her wicked, wicked husband
(crazed by drink and gay company) in a madhouse? It is true that an obtuse jury, misled by the
jesuitical oratory of Mr. Montague Chambers, and
the illogical summing-up of an incompetent judge
(who ever heard before of this Alexander James
Cockburn, Lord Chief Justice of England?) came
subsequently to the conclusion that the naughty
crockery-dealer wasn't mad ; that his wife hadn't
any right to lock him up; and that the medical
gentleman had made rather a blunder in certify-
ing to his insanity ; but what was that manifestly
erroneous verdict, or even the hundred and fifty
pounds damages which accompanied it, compared
with the public revelation of the great principle,
that a lady who does not love her lord may, after
twenty-eight years of married life, pop him into
a strait-jacket, and have him clapped up in Bedlam? No; not in Bedlam. I retract. In that
admirable and mercifully-conducted Institution,
honorable alike to the Corporation of London
and to the wise and good physicians who watch
over its unhappy inmates (one good man and
true, Dr. Charles Hood, has just been succeeded
by another as true and as good, Dr. Helps), a

case such as that of the crockery-dealer's would
be impossible. There is but one man in the
lunatic wards of Bedlam who is sane (E. O., pot-
boy, 1840), and he must needs lie in hold during
"her Majesty's pleasure ;" for has he not committed the unpardonable sin on earth ?

So long as there are physicians simple enough
to be gulled by the tales of untamable shrews,
or careless enough to grant certificates of insanity
without proper inquiry, so long our better halves
will have a terrible weapon in their hands. This
awful power, which is to be exercised apparently
by those who have the longest tongues and the
greatest faculty for plausible representation,
should serve to keep us men-folks in order.
"Take heed of the axe," cried King Charles on
the scaffold, when a *gobemouche* was sillily hand-
ling the instrument of death. Take heed of the
mufflers and the padded room, O you Bluebeard
husbands. Not only "drink and gay company,"
but bad temper, bad language, tearing down
wall-paper, objecting to doctors prying about the
house, may all be construed into symptoms of
raging madness. I intend to be very careful, in
future, as to the criticisms I pass upon the com-
ponent parts of my Breakfast in Bed. Not a
word about the eggs, about the musty, musty
bacon, about the weakness of the tea, the leatheri-
ness of the toast, the absolute absence of the

4*

muffins! No ebullitions of passion at the tardy
response to the often-tugged bell; no raging or
roaring because the newspapers have not arrived!
In olden time, a birchen rod was hung up in the
best-regulated nurseries, to frighten the little
masters and misses into propriety. In imagination, now, a strait-waistcoat occupies the place on
the wall opposite my pillow, erst filled by the
martyrology; and once a week, when I open my
"Punch," I expect to find that Mr. Shirley Brooks
has made an end of all the bickerings of the
Naggletons by the deportation of Mr. Naggleton
to Munster House, at the requisition of Mrs. N.,
backed by a certificate from Peter Grievous.
What delightful domestic dialogues are those
which take place between the Naggletons! How
infinitely superior to " Mrs. Caudle's Curtain Lectures!" Douglas Jerrold (a sadly over-rated man,
my love) had no knowledge of the world, no wit,
no humor, no insight into character, no loving
tenderness for the foibles of humanity. In the
"Caudle Lectures" he could only show us a vulgar, quick-tempered, aggravating, but thoroughly
good-hearted woman, who scolded her husband
frequently, but loved him dearly. Caudle and
his wife used to wrangle and make it up again;
and, as times go, I dare say were as happy a
couple as could be found between Camberwell
and Chelsea

But a new prophet has arisen. A marvellous painter of manners comes forward to show us a sarcastic, sullen man, half-hyena, half-bear, caged with a tigress of a woman. They abuse one another, they bandy cruel epithets, they hate each other; and I have little doubt that, but for the commendable reticence of the narrator, we could be informed that Mrs. Naggleton throws knives at Mr. Naggleton, and that Mr. N. boxes Mrs. N.'s ears.

This is charming. I like to read "The Naggletons" in bed. Their dialogues add a zest to my bread and butter. I call them Mustard and Cresswell. I had yet to learn that the lives led by the affluent middle-classes in England were of a nature akin to those which one might suppose to be led by the Devils of the Pit; nagging, nagging, jeering, and snarling for ever and ever. I am thankful that I don't belong to the affluent middle-classes, but to the "lower middle ones;" and I am pretty well, I thank you.

Of course the Naggletons are mad—as clearly off their heads as that poor ambassador who, the other night, at Rome, walked in his night-gown into a dining-room full of royal and noble company, demanded in tones of fury to know what the Prince and Princesses were doing there, and ordered them to decamp.

By the way, didn't John Hunter, the famous surgeon, once do something of the same kind? Didn't he come home weary and faint from dissecting or lecturing, and find that his wife had convened a large company for a "quiet evening and a little music;" whereat cried honest John, "Turn all these catamarans out of the house, and bring me my night-gown and slippers!"

Imagine how the Volscians were fluttered; how the scrapers and tinklers levanted; how spinet, harpsichord, theorbo, and viol di gamba were hushed; how the "catamarans" retreated, darting withering looks at this uncivil old sawbones. "A brute of a husband," was this most humane, enlightened, and upright man most probably pronounced; and I only wonder that Mrs. Hunter didn't have him seized on the spot for a maniac. For he was mad, of course.

Thus, then, having arrived at this comfortable conclusion, I lay down the newspapers edited by mad journalists, and ere I ring the bell for Crazy Jane the servant to bring up hot water— the mad barber who is to shave my head isn't come yet—I ponder in my darkened mind as to who the sane people on this harum-scarum ball may be.

Do your duty in your state of life, work hard, live temperately, fare coarsely, give of your store to the poor, fear God, honor the Queen, and train up your children in the way they should go; and Dr. A. may want to feel your pulse and inspect your tongue; Dr. B. tap his forehead, and, looking at you, murmur, "Something wrong there;" Dr. C. ask you how many legs a sheep has; and Dr. D. consign you, by certificate, to a madhouse.

The only way in which I can discern the possibility of establishing sanity is to be a dullard and a fool. Then, all the doctors will swear that you are not only in your senses, but a very wise man; and you may hope in time to be made a K.G., or Governor-General of the Fortunate Islands. Who knows what eminence we may be hoisted to by the time we begin to drivel?

My people won't let me read Dr. Forbes Winslow's big book; but I got, long ago, the opening paragraph by heart, and they cannot rob me of *that*. 'Tis a quintette of wise aphorisms by Hippocrates, in Greek—I forbear to quote the Attic, in mercy to the compositors and the critics—and runs thus: "Life is short; Art, long; the Occasion fleeting; Experience fallacious; Judgment difficult." From which I perpend: young Mr. Wyndham, George Francis Train, Captain Atcherly, Mrs. Cottle, Monsieur Veuillot, and Billy Barlow, are all sane; but

Joseph Garibaldi, Michael Faraday, John Stuart
Mill, and Victor Hugo, are as mad as the Man
in the Moon;—and we don't know anything at
all about it.

ON THINGS GOING, GOING—GONE!

WHAT will they pull down, root up, cut through, or trample upon next? I asked myself yesterday, throwing down the newspaper on the counterpane. It isn't alone our old institutions. *They* have gone by the board long ago, of course. It isn't alone the framework of society or the guarantees of morality. Of course, *they* have all disappeared since the Reform Bill was passed, and the Eleventh of George the Second enacted that law-pleadings were to be drawn no more in Latin, and the Test and Corporation Acts were abolished. But the terrible thing is in this pulling down London about our ears. Here am I, tranquilly Breakfasting in Bed this morning; but how do I know but that the ground-landlord is not hungering to make a *tabula rasa* of a quiet street of Russell Square, and build a row of staring shops or bran new banking-houses in lieu of the present row of dingy middle-class mansions, in one of which a discontented scribbler, with a deranged liver, is gnawing dry toast in bed? Up and down the weary columns of the paper do mine eyes travel, and their way is through a desert of demolitions with scarcely an oasis of stability. Underground Railway, forsooth! Thames Embankment, quotha! Main Drainage, save the mark! Strand Hotel, Adelphi Hotel, Charing-Cross Hotel—hotels everywhere and anywhere, and a murrain to them! New streets built, old streets swept away. Where are we all going to? Why can't they leave things as they are?

To keep "things as they are" is understood to be one of the chief maxims of that great Conservative reaction popular among that very numerous class who, having got on in the world and made their fortunes by repeated changes and innovations, are anxious for an era of immutable rest, in order that they may keep what they have acquired. I don't wonder at the kind of contemptuous pity with which politicians speak of "an ancient Whig." Is there not, indeed, something very nearly approaching senility in professing Liberal opinions when you have gotten your desire—a title, a gold stick, a commissionership of excise, a county-court judgeship, or something else nice and comfortable, worth a thousand a year and upwards? Radicalism, Liberalism, are all very well to chalk your shoes with as you climb up the rungs of the ladder; but, the top one attained, there is nothing like a boot of good strong Conservative leather to kick the ladder and the people clinging to it down, withal.

Next to keeping things as they are, the favorite doctrine of your genuine true-blue Reactionists is, to restore "things as they used to be." I declare that it is quite refreshing to watch the phases of the mania for restoration : from illuminating, to "the old art of tatting;" from the hoop-petticoats of 1745, and the round hats of 1813, to stained-glass windows and old Saxon fonts and columniated pulpits, irreverently called "parson coolers." Let us patch up the old churches, chapter-houses, guest-halls, and rood-screens, by all means. There is nothing new under the sun ; and it may be, "things as they used to was" are infinitely preferable to things as they are. We have gone back to Hessian boots. Why shouldn't we revert to cocked hats and pigtails?

The English language, as at present written, or, as the Danish journalist lately described it, "the rich and sweet and mighty largely latinized Scandinavian dialect," is denounced by sapient critics as a mass of affectations and euphemisms.

Let us return, O my literary brethren, to the "sounding Saxon" of our ancestors, as written by Sir John Cheke in his version of St. Matthew's Gospel, or talk Norse with Dr. Dasent. Restore the old; scoff at the new. *Stare per antiquas*

vias should be our motto. Old clothes are the
only wear. I hear that old Madeira is much
asked for; only, as the wine in question has become almost as rare as a black tulip or a blue
diamond, the cunning wine-merchants are compelled to minister to the public demand for antiquity by fabricating old Madeira from New
South African.

Pray mark how eagerly the newspapers give
insertion to the arguments put forward by the
advocates for the fine old methods of treating
criminals. Hurrah for the jolly old gallows, the
fine old cat-o'-nine-tails, and the noble pillory,
the stocks, the ducking-stool, and the *jougs!* I
yet live in hopes to see a garotter flogged at the
cart's-tail from Langham Place to the Duke of
York's Column.

I have a friend who wants all the ticket-of-
leave men hanged. Why not?—why not break
them on the wheel, burn, or fry, or flay them
alive? They used to do so in the good old times.
And what a pestilent, meddling, prying Radical
of a fellow was that Jack Howard—a plague on
all philanthropists, say I—who found out that if
felons' gaols were not made clean and airy and
wholesome, and if that terrible doom, depriva-
tion of the liberty of *going whither a man wills,*
were not compensated for by wholesome and regular food, prisons would become the filthiest of

Augean stables, with fine old fevers and agues careering about, for the benefit of so many wild beasts and so many maniacs.

The worst of the matter is, that with all your mending, restoring, and preserving labors, things *won't* keep as they are, and obstinately refuse to return to that which they used to be. 'Tis like an old hat that has been " molokered," or ironed and greased into a simulacrum of its pristine freshness ; or an old coat that has been black-and-blue revivered. For a day or two all is well, and the daw may strut about in his pea-cock's feathers, the envy of the entire farm-yard ; but the first shower of rain washes off the ficti-tious gloss, and scrubs the whitening off the se-pulchre, and exposes all the senility and shabbi-ness of the sham.

You may bring the corpse of Antiquity to Surgeons' Hall, and galvanize its stark limbs into a hideous semblance of vitality ; but the spark once fled, not all the Leyden jars in the world shall make that mass of dead dough sentient. Better macerate the flesh from off the bones, and hang up the skeleton in a museum, ere it crum-bles into the dust from which it came. You see that, in a lofty rostrum, high up above us all, and our miserable sphere of power, there is a certain Great Auctioneer, who uses now his scythe, and now his hour-glass, for a hammer;

and he—whose name is Time—brings all things human to public Roup, and sells them by inch of corpse-candle. For ever does he from his clattering jaw cry, "Going, going—gone!"

"Going, going!"—put money in thy purse,—tick your catalogue with pencil-marks,—bid with wild haste,—fee agents and brokers,—catch the auctioneer's eye till it coruscates with nods and winks, when—thump!—down goes the hammer on the pulpit-ledge, and you find that the thing for which your desire lay and your soul was adrought is gone for ever. Gone whither, it is bootless, now, to inquire.

I hold it for certain that few persons ever went to a sale to buy a certain thing, and were permitted to purchase precisely the article they longed for. Something is knocked down to them,—and dear is the price it has been run up to—but it is not the particular object. And so it is always. You get *a* wife, but not *the* wife. You are made Chief-Justice at Timbuctoo, not Attorney-General at the Cameroons; and it is all one in the end.

"Going, going—gone!" London is going even while I pen these lines—going in despite of topographical Conservatives who wish to keep things as they are, and archæological revivalists who strive to resuscitate things as they used to be. Westminster Hall is itself, and more than itself again; and William Rufus might wag his shock red head with joy to look upon its wondrous roof, brave painted window, noble dais, and towering brass candelabra; St. Stephen's has cloisters once more, and, underground, its crypt has been cleared out; all over the metropolis we hear of churches being restored, Lady-chapels revivified, and palaces renovated.

The reverse to this flattering medal is in the pig-headed determination evinced in some quarters to keep the bad old things—the filthy streets, the bulging rotten tenements, the haunts of felons and vagrants, the abominable old nuisances and obstructions—as they are. Eight years ago I strove hard, in a journal called "Household Words," and in an essay entitled "Gibbet Street," to make the respectable classes aware of what a hideous, pestilential, fever, thief, and beggar infested place was Charles Street, Drury Lane; and how it was a hot-bed and forcing-house for the hulks and the scaffold.

I remark that recently "S. G. O.," in the "Times," has been sailing (in the wind of indifference's teeth) on the same tack, and, under the generic term of "Guilt Gardens," has exposed the misery and the shame of these places. Yet do I fear that Charles Street, Drury Lane, and its congeners, will outlive both Lord Sidney Godolphin Osborne and his humble protest.

I have not yet heard anything about pulling
down the Coal Yard, Church Lane, St. Giles's, or
Dudley Street, or those most scandalous little ar-
teries injected with the worst of human blood
that stagnate and fester, varicose in their vagabondism, about Gray's Inn Lane. And Middle
Row, Holborn? and Clement's Lane, Strand?
and the *cloaca* of Clare Market? and the Colonnade behind Guildford Street, Russell Square?
These frightful dens yet exist, yet flourish in rank
luxuriance; and any number of vested interests
would shrink with indignant affright were it proposed to pull them down. Proposed!

In my mind's eye I can see a phlegmatic-look-
ing gentleman, in a well buttoned frock-coat,
smoking his cigarette in his *cabinet de travail* at
the Tuileries, and, as he emits curling threads of
blue vapor, or twists his spiky moustache, going
over a map of Paris; then placing his imperial
finger on a labyrinth of slums, he says sharply to
Baron Haussmann, "*M. le Prefét, ôtez moi ce
tas d'immondices*"—sweep me all this rubbish
away before the name of Robinson (hight Jack)
can be thrice pronounced. But, then, my friend,
I should not like to give up my *Habeas Corpus*,
and my right to good and substantial bail—with
sundry other trifles light as air in the way of
liberty—for the sake of getting rid of the Coal
Yard or Middle Row.

The transformation of London, of which the commencement may be dated from the attainment of his majority by the Prince of Wales, will be necessarily slow and gradual; for we have no Prefects of the Thames—our municipal authorities are more retrogressive than progressive, and it would be easier, I take it, to obtain a grant of City money for furbishing up the Lord Mayor's coach, or replacing the rotten portals of Temple Bar, than for laying out Smithfield as a Park, or sweeping away the nasty purlieus of Finsbury.

Yet even within the charmed circle wherein William the King, six hundred years ago, told William the Bishop and Godfrey the Portreve that all citizens should be law-worthy, and all children be their father's heirs after their father's days—even within the domains of Gog and Magog, there are numerous signs of a " Going, going—gone !" era.

Temple Bar, it is true, stands as fast as the barber's on one side and the banking-house on the other can make it; but Chancery Lane has been widened, and handsome edifices substituted for the queer, tumble-down, albeit picturesque old tenements, of which the only records now are the etchings of John Thomas Smith.

Messrs. Adams and Ede the robe-makers, Partridge and Cozens the stationers, and the London

Restaurant, have given a very different aspect to the Fleet Street corners of the Lane—which, however, becomes antique enough as you progress northward, the fat, legal spiders interlacing their webs from Lincoln's Inn to Clifford and Sergeant's Inn—and to hives of chambers yet consecrated to dirt and dust and dryrot, the concoction of demurrers, and the spinning of special pleas.

Is there not likewise Symond's Inn, that backyard of the law, that wretched little *cour des miracles* of twentieth-rate legal practitioners, where dubious articled clerks borrow admitted attorneys' names to grace their dusky panels, and the writ with which you are served by Spinks is issued in the name of Jinks? Who is the phantom Jinks—this stalking-horse, this parchment ægis of the unqualified pettifogger, this plastron of Tidd's practice—is he alive or dead? Does he call for the rent of his name regularly? Does he look in at Symond's Inn from time to time, to see how his double is getting on? Does the appellation he lets out on hire belong really to the fiend, like Peter Schlemil's shadow? Some of these days, Symond's—the least known, perhaps, of all the obscure Inns of Chancery—must go by the board; and it is, even now, an anachronism. I always fancy it the haunt of the last professors of the art of forestalling, regrating, and common barratry; of old-world lawyers, who yet sue by mesne process, the Eleventh of George the Second notwithstanding, draw pleadings in Latin, and frame answers in Norman-French.

I always look for the names of John Doe or Richard Roe on the door-jambs; or expect to find John a' Nokes arguing in the centre of the court-yard with John a' Styles on the vexed question of the pied horses and the horses that were pied.

But hie we through the bar again.; or better still, thread one of those astounding mazes of dirty lanes, full of chandlers' shops, bookstalls, law-writers, beggars, marine stores, fried-fish, and furniture brokers, that lie between Carey Street and Clare Market. Glance at the filthy bye streets which recall the famous names of Denzil Holles, of the Earl of Clare, of the Duchess of Newcastle. Struggle down, as well as you can for costermongers' barrows and sprawling children, past Wych Street, and ere you come into the Strand, and to Holywell Street, look to the gaping space to the left. That Sahara of rubbish, girt by a fringe of crumbling brickwork, was once Lyon's Inn.

"On the subject of Lyon's Inn," writes Ireland, "all historians remain silent." I wonder that the distinguished papa of the Shakesperian forger, and who was himself by no means remarkable for veracity, did not think it worth his while

5

to fill up the historic vacuum which he laments, by means of a few lies. When Sam Ireland, senior, visited Lyon's Inn in the first year of the present century, he found the Hall (which was built in 1700) destitute of any circumstance to recommend it save its extreme filth, and opines that the use of mops and brooms was totally unknown to the principal and ancients of this honorable society. A brood of chickens was tranquilly roosting on the *haut pas*, and an old hen was laying down the law to an attentive audience of cobwebs.

And yet this inconceivably dingy and decayed old place had been, according to the steward's account, an Inn of Chancery since the days of Henry V. I can imagine Sir John Falstaff lodging there, and being dunned for the rent of his chambers when Mrs. Quickly declined to afford him any more accommodation on trust at the Boar's Head. Ireland gives an etching of it, which may be found in his "History of the Inns of Court." It was in truth a very kennel, a cave of Adullam, whither repaired all that were in debt and all that were discontented. I wonder that it was not converted into a furniture bazaar, for from year's end to year's end the brokers were always "in" some one or other of the chambers; as for the tenants, those who were not bankrupt were profligate—there was always somebody down with low fever, and always somebody else up with *delirium tremens*. Lyon's Inn, as to its occupancy, was a receiving-house for the Insolvent Debtors' Court, and an ante-chamber to Whitecross Street. Still had the unlovely little place its *fasti*—not very pleasant, but memorable ones nevertheless. Is it not recorded by Lockhart, in his ballad on the Gill's Hill Lane murder, that the victim's name was "Mr. William Weare," and that he "dwelt in Lyon's Inn"? Yes; in one of those mouldy sets of chambers lived the disreputable sharper and "mace man," who was only thwarted in his scheme to plunder three rogues by the three rogues aforesaid laying a plot, more cunning, more desperate, and more successful, for plundering him. The booty was a wretched one—not a tithe of what they expected; but Mr. Jack Thurtell—who I am given to understand was a rollicking boon companion, and only second as a convivial vocalist to his admired associate Mr. Hunt—was a gentleman who would have meal if he could not get malt, and in default of either, blood; so that, in default of spoil, he very punctually murdered Mr. William Weare.

That Lyon's Inn should have any connection with the First Napoleon may, at the first blush, appear strange and improbable. In a visit of the present Ruler of France in the old days,

when he was "Prince Bonyparty," the needy
adventurer, to whom wiseacres would scarcely
allow any wits to live upon, there would have
been little out of the way.   He might have gone
to Lyon's Inn to get a little bill done, or to pay
the interest on one that was overdue.   But Napoleon the Great, Emperor and King and Pro-
tector of the Confederation of the Rhine ! what
could he have had to do with the shady little
Inn nestling in the purlieus of the Strand?
Thus much: John Wilson Croker, the late
Secretary to the Admiralty, literary squidfish of
the " Quarterly Review," and friend of the
Marquis of Hertford, in his celebrated endeavor
to whitewash Sir Hudson Lowe, blacken the
memory of Napoleon, and squelch Barry
O'Meara, tells (Oct. 1822) a sufficiently curious
story, setting forth how, a short time before his
(O'Meara's) departure from St. Helena, a ship
arrived from England, having on board a box
of French books and a letter addressed to a Mr.
Fowler, the partner of Mr. Balcombe, Buona-
parte's purveyor.   Mr. Fowler, on opening the
letter, found that it contained nothing but an
enclosure addressed to *James Forbes, Esq.*   As
he knew no James Forbes, he thought it his
duty to carry the letter to the Governor ; further inquiries ascertained that there was no person of the name of James Forbes on the Island ;

and accordingly it was thought proper to open this mysterious letter before the Governor and Council, when it was found to begin with the words "Dear O'Meara;" it was dated *Lyon's Inn, London,* and signed *William Holmes.* And to think that Mr. William Holmes may be yet alive, while I am Breakfasting in Bed! 'Tis but forty years since; Mr. Holmes may have begun business early. Who shall say but that the placid, white-haired old gentleman I saw yesterday contemplating the ruins of Lyon's Inn was Mr. William Holmes, come to a green old age, and serenely unmindful of the dark, tempestuous time when he was the occult agent of the Captive of St. Helena, when he wrote: "I expect to hear from my friends at Rome and Munich, of which you shall have due information?" Rome and Munich were then the residence of the banished princes and princesses of the Imperial family, of Eugène Beauharnais and Cardinal Fesch.

Again writes the sibylline Holmes: "The 100,000 francs, lent in 1816, are paid; likewise the 72,000 francs, which complete the 395,000 francs mentioned on the 15th March. The 36,000 francs for 1817, and the like sum for 1819, have also been paid by the person ordered. Remain quiet as to the funds placed; the farmers are good, and they will pay bills for the amount of the income, which must be calculated at the rate of four per cent."

"Going, going—gone !" William Holmes may
have been an old, old man, ere he was trusted
with the secrets of the Napoleonic finance, and
may have slept the last sleep these thirty years.
He and his mysteries, and the Inn he transacted
his business in, all fade away into a mass of
crumbling rubbish, to be carted away, leaving
no vestige behind.

And Exeter 'Change—not the 'Change of Pid-
cock and Crosse, and poor Chunee the Elephant,
but the more modern structure—the lamentable
arcade where none but crazy or impecunious
tenants could be found for the dingy little dens
of shops : of that, too, must be written *fuit*. And
Hungerford Market, with Mr. Gatti's ice-shop !
The Market is gone, and the Bridge likewise.
The adage is reversed, and the fish has become
fleshified.

There : I have no heart to read about any more
metropolitan improvements. The London of the
past, the London of my youth, the London in
which I can remember the dancing bear and the
camel with the monkey on his back, the climbing
boys and the small-coal man, Padlock House,
and Cranbourn Alley, Chalk Farm and the Holy
Land, the Borough Mint and George the Fourth's
statue at King's Cross, the Mews and Cotton Garden, the Quadrant Colonnade and the Thatched
House Tavern—this London has disappeared for

ever. What next, I wonder? Is Temple Bar to suffer the common lot? Does any bold iconoclast contemplate the removal of Middle Row? Is the integrity of St. Martin's Workhouse threatened? Or will it occur to an innovating Duke of Bedford that Russell Square, laid out as a public pleasure-garden, and surrounded by handsome mansions and hotels, with shops and *cafés* on the basement, might be made one of the most magnificent *places* in Europe? Who knows?

Meanwhile I turn on my pillow, and, taking up the supplement to the "Times," observe with grim satisfaction that a twenty-one years' lease of a house in Golden Square is to be sold. Aha! that choice resort of the dinginesses and the second-handisms is safe for nearly a quarter of a century. It will last my time, and the worms will be Breakfasting on me, in *my* Bed, ere the sepulchral cry of "Going, going—gone!" is heard over Golden Square!

ON BEING BURNT ALIVE.

WE have all of us, I deferentially infer, dreamt some strange and curious and horrible things in our time—not necessarily after a supper of under-done pork-chops, but often under calm and placid outward circumstances, which one might naturally assume to be conducive to the most balmily-tranquil slumbers. I went to-bed the other night, with nothing particular on my conscience, and after no cœnal meal heavier than three pills. I woke up in the gray of the morning in an agony of terror, for I had dreamt that I was Burnt Alive.

Not merely condemned to the stake or delivered over to the secular arm. No, no, no! I was actually and corporally (in my dream) consumed by Fire. A fearsome thing!

In that heterogeneous medley of humor, buffoonery, eloquence, poetry, pathos, Scotch egotism and conceit, blind Toryism, abstract Republicanism, wit, gluttony, scurrility, philosophy, and drunkenness, the "Noctes Ambrosianæ," Professor Wilson makes the Ettrick Shepherd relate his experience, in a dream, of the gallows.

Mr. Timothy Tickler expresses his opinion that to dream of being hanged is a luxury; but the Shepherd sees nothing at all luxurious in it.

"It's the warst job of a'," says the mythical James Hogg, "and gars my very sowl sicken wi' horror for sake o' the puir deevils that's really hang'd out and out, *bonâ fide*, wi' a tangible tow, and a hangman that's mair than a mere apparition; a pardoned felon, wi' creeshy second-hand corduroy breeks, and coat short at the cuffs, sae that his thick hairy wrists are visible when he's adjustin' the halter; hair red, red, yet no sae red as his bleared een, glarin' wi' an unaccountable fierceness."

This is undeniably graphic, but too imaginative. The Shepherd had evidently never come in contact with the real hangman—the demure, highly respectable, Methodist-parson-looking man, who executes with quiet docorum the dread mandate of the law, and turns you off gingerly, for fear of spoiling your clothes, which he is going to sell to Madame Tussaud for the Chamber of Horrors.

Mr. Hogg, however, was not satisfied with being hanged. It occurred to him to dream that he was beheaded. The ceremony took place on a scaffold, forty feet high, "a' hung wi' black cloth, and open to a' airts." The headsman was "sax feet and some inches" high. He stood "wi'

5*

an axe over his shoulder, and his twa naked arms
o' a fearsome thickness, a' crawlin' wi' sinews, like
a yard o' cable to the sheet-anchor o' a man-o'-
war." The executioner, it appears, turned squeam-
ish over the task of cutting Mr. Hogg's head off.
"The axe fell out o' his hauns, and, bein' sharp,
its ain wecht drav' it quiverin' into the block, and
close to my ear; the verra senseless wood gied a
groan. I louped up on to my feet. I cried wi'
a loud voice, ' Countrymen, I stand here for the
sacred cause of Liberty all over the world.' . . . .
I might have escaped; but I was resolved to
cement the cause with my martyred blood. I
was not a man to disappoint the people. They
had come there to see me die"—not James Hogg
the Ettrick Shepherd, but Hogg the Liberator
—" and from my blood, I felt assured, would
arise millions of armed men, under whose tread
would sink the thrones of ancient dynasties, and
whose hand would unfurl to all the winds the
standard of Freedom, never again to encircle the
staff till its dreadful rustling had quailed the
kings—even as the mountain sough sends down
upon their knees whole herds of cattle, ere rattles from summit to summit the exulting music
of the thunder-storm."

This is very fine and grand, and piles up the
agony with a vengeance; but still I don't believe very strongly that worthy James Hogg ever

had such a dream or dreams. The narrative was probably written by the eloquent Professor Wilson, not when "aiblins fou" at Mr. Ambrose's in Picardy Place, but with calm deliberation in his own study. As a rule, you may make certain that the circumstances under which celebrated literary exercitations are said to have been composed are not those which actually occurred; and, equally as a rule, you may rest satisfied that the scenes and characters most elaborately drawn and most minutely filled up are those with which the author has had the slightest personal acquaintance.

For all that, I really am Breakfasting in Bed this morning, and I positively did dream last night that I was being Burnt Alive.

It was terrible. I really felt the crackling agony of the flames. Schoolboys often dream of being flogged; but the bodily is not commensurate with the mental pain, and the shadowy pedagogue's blows fall lightly as those of a bladder filled with peas. I have dreamt of being devoured by wild beasts, but always woke as they were beginning to crunch my bones, and before they got to the marrow; of drowning; of suffocation by charcoal; and especially of *being buried alive.* Arrah! that horrible hot atmosphere of the coffin, and the grave-clothes that swaddle and hamper you as you kick for freedom, and the dreadful pressure of the coffin-lid on your nose ; while all the while you are visually conscious of the gravedigger smoking a pipe and drinking cold rum-and-water with your mother-in-law in the parlor of the Half-Moon and Seven Stars, the third house to the left round the corner as you leave the cemetery !

" He wa'n't of much account," says the gravedigger, burying his nose in the rum-and-water.

" He was a black-hearted villain," adds your mother-in-law, filling her second pipe.

What a disturbance the old lady used to make if you ventured on a mild havanna in the back drawing-room ! And then you begin kicking again in your shroud and cerements, and—you wake !

I didn't wake for hours, so it seemed—for hours, for weeks, for months, for years, for centuries—while I was being burnt alive. The Inquisition did it all, of course. "In half an hour from the first spark the hills glowed with fire unextinguishable by a waterspout. The crackle became a glow, as acre after acre joined the flames. Here and there a rock stood in the way, and the burning waves broke against it, till the crowning birch-tree took fire, and its leaves, like a shower of flaming diamonds, were in a minute consumed." Well, it wasn't like *that*. "Millions and millions of sparks of fire in heaven, but only some six or seven stars. How calm the large lustre of Hesperus!" Certainly; only Hesperus didn't shine when I was burnt alive. Not only sparks, but stars, whole constellations, with any number of suns, moons, and comets to boot, danced before my eyes. Not only my body, but my brain was on fire. I was bound to the stake, or the bedpost, or something of that sort. I think that at one stage of my agony I was a Hindoo widow in the performance of the rite of suttee, with plenty of flax and fresh butter to keep me blazing, and a Brahmin gentleman, with a fine yellow streak of caste on his forehead, to assure me of eternal felicity immediately after my reduction to a cinder. Then I was transformed into a cat, and an enormous gorilla held me tight in one hairy arm, while with the other he guided my unwilling paw to sweep some chestnuts off a red-hot hob. Then, of course, in the usual manner of digressional dreaming, I ran off at several tangents, and became Sir Edwin Landseer, M. Paul de Chaillu, and the late Mr. Douglas Jerrold's comedy of "The Cat's-paw;" but I was still burning, and so continued to burn, till I could feel and writhe no longer—when I awoke.

It is a gruesome thing to have undergone these torments even in a dream. *Deja!* Prince Talleyrand might have remarked, had I subjected

my fiery feelings to the most obvious and most
usual degree of comparison.

Of course I know what it all arose from. It
wasn't indigestion. It wasn't liver. It wasn't
determination of blood to the head ; and I don't
think it was conscience. 'Twas merely the incoherent embodiment of an imagination excited by
the perusal of those dreadful accounts of young
girls being burnt alive, of which we have had
lately a melancholy succession. I had been reading about the catastrophe at Nice ; about the
grim tragedy of the transformation-scene at the
Princess's Theatre ; about the accident in Harley
Street; about Doctor Lankester, the coroner, and
his indignant philippics against crinoline. I had
gone to bed with my head full of the poor suf-
ferers who had been burnt alive, and sleep had
knitted up the ravelled skein of preoccupation
into a dire fabric of disasters to myself.

One has but to glance from column to column
of the papers to breakfast—if you forswear supping—full of horrors. Burnt alive! Burnt
alive! Burnt alive! the catalogue goes on in
lurid iteration. The poor have woes enough of
their own, God knows; but this is an anguish
of which the rich, so far from being exempt, seem
the chosen and particular victims.

Youth and beauty, carriages and horses, live-
ried servants, rank, brave garments, lip-service,

and homage, shall not wrest Lady Clara Vere de
Vere from the clutch of the Fire Demon.   Let
her paint an inch thick, and to the complexion
of charred and greasy ashes she comes—comes
through insensate vanity and recklessness.   The
music of the ball is yet rippling in soft waves of
sound through her ears; the sugared compliments of her cavaliers still, half-melted, leave a
dulcet velvet-pile on her lips; she is spreading
out the radiant finery in which she has fluttered
through the festival.   Poor little ephemeral fash-
ion-gnat!   The flounces and furbelows which
have made so many men enthusiastic, so many
women jealous, still rustle round her, diaphanous
and fluent, when all is changed to a dreadful flare
and crackling.   Like Facinata in her burning
tomb, she writhes in a shroud of flame.   The mili-
ner's handiwork is beaten into powder by the
Cinder Fiend.   There is nothing left but scorched
and naked limbs.

And when the Fire comes, reprehending no
vanity, placing his brand of interdict on no preposterous frenzy of fashion, but dipping his finger
into the family wine-cup and setting it flaming,
starting up from the cozy hearth, leaping like a
treacherous beast of blood from out the bars of
the grate—how is it then?   When we were children, we used to nickname the live cinders that
fell from the fire, to the imminent peril of the

hearth-rug, "purses" or "coffins." The first,
when cold and shaken, had a pleasant money-
jingling sound. The last had an ugly longitudi-
nal form; and the morbid-minded among us declared we could discern on the surface ominous
little specks and spots, that were at once assumed
to represent a coffin-plate and nails.

Those leaping biers are grimly common just
now. They disdain to smoulder in the woollen
rug before the hearth. Their favorite resting-
place is in the gauzy folds of the lady's dress.
The coffins gape, they have grown into sepul-
chres, and folly falls into them.

I said the rich seemed marked out specially for
such torment. Ah, vain and presumptuous assertion! Ah, crudest of dogmatisms! Who is
exempt from aught? That workhouse pauper is
a martyr to the same lumbago which makes rigid
the loins of the million-rich banker. The Fire
may oftentimes seem spitefully faithful to afflu-
ence, as though he said, "Aha! I will show them
that money-bags shall not avail against live coals.
Oho! I will prove that my furnace has a red-
der hue than Burke's Peerage. Aï! aï! I will
teach them to have balls, and banquets, and junk-
etings." But he comes back at last to the stern,
impartial rule; and he who is own brother to Death
proclaims himself, like Death, mighty and just.
Question not the equity of the Fire King's dis-

pensation.   All he touches with red-hot sceptre:
you, and me, and all the world.   Who of us, in
his calendar of griefs, cannot recall some horrible
red-letter days?

When this old hat was new, it was encircled
by a crape; and for whom worn?—the little,
little kinsman, with his dark eyes, and merry
laugh, and bright face, that made us remember,
half-joyfully, half-tearfully, the lineaments of the
dear dead that had gone before him.   And he
was playing before the fire in the upper room,
when, with that cruel carelessness which makes
us almost think some girls to be fiends, the servant had left him—left him on some idle chattering errand.   And his pinafore caught fire; and
there was an inquest—a grave judicial investiga-
tion—on that poor little morsel of humanity.
And—look you here, my brother.   If we were
all to mourn for ever and aye, and to refuse to
be comforted, and to parade our grief before all
the world, do you think this same world could
go on?   Do you think that He, whose wisest
creature told us that "joy cometh in the morning," would not have cause to cast us away as
selfish and ungrateful?

We read in the Book to which Dr. Cocker-
Colenso has taken so many arithmetical objec-
tions, that when the child that Uriah's wife bare
to David was stricken with sickness, the king be-

sought God for the child, and fasted, and went in and lay all night upon the earth, refusing to eat bread, or to be raised up by the elders of his house; when on the seventh day the child died, and his servants feared to tell him. He nevertheless discovered, from their scared looks, that the little one was lost; and then "*arose from the earth, and washed and anointed himself, and changed his apparel, and came into the house of the Lord and worshipped: then he came to his own house; and when he required, they set bread before him, and he did eat;*" answering, when his servants marvelled at the strange change in his behavior, "*While the child was yet alive, I fasted and wept; for I said, Who can tell whether God will be gracious to me, that the child may live? But now he is dead, wherefore should I fast? Can I bring him back again? I shall go to him; but he shall not return to me.*"

These awful accidents by fire, which, with terrible similarity of occurrence, have made us all tremble and stand amazed, have, through that odd yet usual propensity of the English people for imitating the procedure of a bull running at a gate, been laid at the door of crinoline. If ladies did not persist in wearing exaggerated hoop-petticoats, urged the Bull-Run philosophers, there would be no catastrophes from fire. I don't think such nonsense was ever talked out of Bedlam ; yet you find plenty of people, ordinarily supposed to be sensible and even sagacious, who join in this parrot-cry. 'Tis on a par, for common sense, with the silly dogmatists among the " practical " penal philosophers, who are for having all criminals, whatsoever may be their offence, starved, flogged, and worked in chain-gangs, merely because their own cowardice and avarice have been aroused and alarmed by the street-outrages of a couple of score garotters. I am not about to cry up crinoline. I am not favored with the acquaintance of any manufacturers of steel-springs and horsehair petticoats, and have no wish to puff the dealers in such articles. Nor am I disposed to deny that unduly bulging skirts have been the cause of numerous accidents by fire or otherwise. But do you think that young, middle-aged, or old ladies would cease to be burnt alive if petticoats were reduced to the circumference in fashion forty years ago, when a lady's dress fell in a perpendicular line close to her limbs from hip to ankle ; when the gown was, in fact, but " a pantaloon on one leg ?" Bah ! dilated crinoline is a nuisance to men, and makes some women very ridiculous; but the real root of the evil in fire-casualties is not crinoline.

When ironmongers abandon the abominable practice of building fashionable grates, of which the topmost bars are scarcely half a foot from the ground, and which present an ever-yawning fiery furnace, from which immaculate virtue would scarcely have saved Shadrach, Meshach, and Abednego; when masters of families sternly in-sist upon every grate in every room being per-manently protected by wire-guards; and when, above all, mothers of families exert their author-ity to prohibit their daughters wearing sleezy gauze and muslin dresses in winter time—we may look for a surcease of suttee in drawing-rooms and parlors. I say this last is a matter which concerns Mater-familias, and her alone. I suppose the British mother has still some power left, notwithstanding the very fast manners of the rising generation. I don't want any cruelty, oppression, tyranny, to carry out the gauze-and-muslin taboo. I only call for a calm and determined expression of maternal will.

When the unsophisticated old lady from Ken-tucky first saw some New York young ladies indulging in the vagaries of the *valse à deux temps,* she very uncompromisingly stated how she would treat *her* daughters if they betook them-selves to such Terpsichorean gambadoes. "I'd give 'em the hickory," this Spartan parent ex-claimed, "if they were as big as Goliath and as old as Methusalem." We know what equally rigid discipline was prescribed by one of the interlocutors in George Colman's "Night-gown and Slippers" for boarding-school misses who addicted themselves to the pernicious practice of novel-reading. Well, we don't want such a Brownrigge system of procedure as this. Only let Mamma say to her daughters, "My dears, you sha'n't be burnt alive, if I can help it; and therefore I won't allow you to wear gauze, tarlatans, or muslins in winter-time."

As for crinoline itself, I am afraid that prohibitions, satiric, nay fierce, denunciations, will, for a time, be powerless against it. The ladies, old as well as young, have nailed their crinoline to the mast; and, if they are determined to wear a certain thing, who shall gainsay them? The Duke of Tantivy's daughters wear top-boots,— tops, madam; mahoganies; *bottes à revers;* "pickle-jars,"—precisely as you choose to employ one or the other more or less euphuistic (I mean slangy) locution. These fair pilasters, whose sire is a pillar of the state, enclose their slender shafts and pediments in the leathern coverings of which the use is ordinarily supposed to be confined to fox-hunters, post-boys, and farmers of the old school. I have it on authority. There is not the slightest compromise in the Duke's daughters' tops. They are *not* gaiters. They are *not* Balmorals prolonged upwardly to preternatural proportions.

My informant is acquainted with the Crispin employed to manufacture these articles for the Duke's daughters. Any fine afternoon during the full Brighton season you may see these young patricians, with their governess; Mdlle. de Cuir-bouilli, on the sea-highway between the Battery (or where, at least, the Battery used, and the new hotel is, to be) and Pool Valley. If the wind be indulging in even the smallest puffs of his char-tered libertinism (and he is scarcely ever on thoroughly good behavior at Brighton), the demurest eye must glance perforce at the shining tops I allude to, pharoses, so to speak, in the surging sea of crinoline.. This is a wonderful age, and we are a wonderful people, and the River Amazon has astounding tributaries in our country.

When I laid out my annual half-a-crown last Christmas—and the outlay is one I trust to be permitted the indulgence of for some years to come—in the purchase of "Punch's Pocket-Book," and surveyed Mr. John Leech's panora-mic etching of "Sea-side Fashions for 1863,"—and when I came upon the group of the fox-hunting-looking belles, in orthodox "pink," lea-thers, boots, and whips,—I could scarcely help exclaiming, "Mr. Leech, Mr. Leech, this is not character but caricature. This is a madness of the pencil, a frenzy of the etching-needle, the hallucination of a humorous draughtsman, embracing his chimera." But, behold, January was yet young, and Nature had hardly manifested her abhorrence for the vacuum caused by the abstraction of the above-mentioned half-a-crown from my pocket, when, on undeniable authority, I was told that the Leechian cartoon was the, graven embodiment, not of a myth, but of a literal truth, and that the Duke of Tantivy's daughters really wore top-boots.

And why not? This is a free country. Sumptuary laws have been abolished for ever so many centuries. Where is the use of having a Habeas Corpus, if portions of the feminine corporate body are not to be thrust with impunity into such boots as caprice may suggest, or convenience dictate, or fashion warrant? I see ladies driving in the Park in paletôts made by Poole. Our wives are ceasing to employ mantle-makers, and beginning to order their coats from their husbands' tailors; this ingenious contrivance having a double purpose — that of increasing your own sartorial accounts, and of giving the dear creatures an opportunity for spending on other finery the ready money which, either by passionate entreaty or gentle coercion, they will extract from you, whether coats or mantles, hats or bonnets, are the wear.

Why not? I repeat. Some years since, our

charmers used to wear shaggy pilot-jackets, with mother-o'-pearl buttons of alarming circumfer- ence, into the pockets of which (the jackets, not the buttons) they were wont to thrust their tiny hands. Don't you remember, again, the waist- coat mania among the ladies—when they dis- covered that long gold chains were utterly use- less, and had, consequently, to be provided with Albert or brequet guards—including, of course, a quantity of " charms "—to secure their watches in their side-pockets? What kind of habiliments did Queen Christina of Sweden patronise ? Why, she dressed like a grenadier. And Joan of Arc ? Why, she wore corslet and greaves, gauntlets and surcoat, like a man-at-arms. To be sure they burnt her alive (or are said to have done so, for many French archæologists maintain that Joan lived to a good old age) for wearing too much crinoline—or plate-armor.

I have read in the autobiography of the Czarina Catherine II., that her predecessor, Elizabeth, when a fat, *passée* dame, very unwieldy, and very fond (too fond) of champagne, was addicted to appearing at the court balls *en cavalier;* that is to say, in a tightly-fitting hussar uniform. A squabby, elderly woman in tights is neither a very edifying nor a very delectable spectacle; but who was to question the sovereign will and pleasure of Elizabeth, the Supreme Empress of

all the Russias, Great Duchess of Moscow, Pro-
tectress of the Republic of Novgorod, and so
forth? The fashions vary, and the ladies please
themselves. *Vive la mode—et la bagatelle!*

Who shall say that Semiramis didn't wear top-
boots; and that Ninus, that celebrated prototype
of the hen-pecked husband, was not county-
courted for the account by the Runciman of the
period? More than a hundred years ago the
beautiful Miss Gunnings were the reigning " sensational " toasts in London ; and they appeared
at the drums and routs of the nobility and gentry attired, or unattired, in the manner of which
the female artistes attached to the *poses plastiques*
have now, without rivalry, a monopoly.

A great French painter once told me that the
wrinkled, snuffy old woman who swept out his
studio was gazing one day upon a picture on his
easel, representing Venus (*costume en chair*, buff
trimmings) rising from the sea. "Ah," she murmured, "*les beaux jours! on se montrait ainsi,
quasi-nue, au ciel, hein? Moi aussi j'ai posé
dans le temps.*" She had filled the part (for a
gratuity of ten francs nine sols) of Goddess of
Reason in Maximilian Robespierre's famous Bed-
lamite pageant, and had been drawn on a tri-
umphal car through the streets of unbelieving
Paris. "What costume did you wear?" asked
the painter. "*Dam! queq' chose comm' ca*"
6

("something like that"), replied the snuffy old
sweeper, pointing to the Venus with nothing to
wear. You see, it was the fashion of those Re-
publican times. The French, in liberty, equality,
fraternity, and other things, outstripped all their
contemporaries.

There is a queer story about the Empress Jose-
phine, when she was the *citoyenne* Beauharnais,
going to a ball at Madame Tallien's in a full suit
of fleshings, and nothing else besides a translucid
and spangled scarf. It was the fashion. The
greatest proficients in made-dishes in the world
began to dress *au naturel*. In 1848 there was a
brief feverish attempt to revive the Goddess-of-
Reason modes; and M. Cham de Noë, I recol-
lect, gave the "Charivari" a humorous sketch,
depicting the Commissary of Police presenting
a blooming young-lady candidate for the office
of *coryphée* at the approaching festival with her
official costume. It was a fig-leaf.

I am inclined, then, to think, on the whole,
that we men-folks talk a great deal of nonsense
in our denunciations of crinoline. It is certain
that ladies were burnt to death centuries before
crinoline was ever heard of; to say nothing of
accidents by fire during the periods when hoop-
petticoats were in abeyance. It is equally certain that the victims to fire-casualties are not the
wearers of silk or woollen-stuff over crinoline ;

but those silly women, young and old, who, through meanness or through vanity, persist in wearing their widely-distended framework with muslins and tarlatans in lieu of stouter fabrics. But the crinoline itself, accepting it as the generic term for hencoops either of horsehair, steel-springs, wire-gauze, cane, or basket-work, I hold to be harmless. The ladies declare it to be eminently pleasant and convenient. The physicians say that it is healthy. There used to be no more painful sight in the streets on rainy days than the ladies holding up their flaccid, drooping, splashed, and draggled coats, in a vain attempt to protect them from the mud-lava and the freshets of the gutter. I suppose ladies are as liable as others folks to rheumatic affections of the limbs, through damp garments clinging to them. I apprehend, the rather, that from this very cause, thousands of hapless women have suffered year after year excruciating agonies, of which we, coarse, selfi h, exigent, intolerant men have never recked. The ladies have a habit of squealing out about trifles, and s ying nothing about real ailments, which last t'ey endure with heroic fortitude and resi nati n. Ah, me! how often the ch ek is quivering underneath the violet powder! How often the blooming English belle is undergoing the anguish of an Indian at the stake!

The lady who wrote in Queen Anne's time to
the editor of the "Spectator," and asked him,
with crushing curtness, what business petticoats
were of his, denied, *à priori*, the right of the
ruder sex to meddle in the criticism of feminine
costume at all. Indeed, I question whether we
have any right to discuss those articles of costume which we merely *see ;* but we are entitled
to say a word or two in praise or dispraise of
those we really *feel.* For example, when the
Sheriff of Middlesex comes down upon us, *àpro-
pos* of Madam's point-lace, parasols, double-
width *glacés*, and innumerable bonnets. We
feel *that*.

Again : when our shins are in a state of per-
manent ecchymosis, from the bobbing and rasp-
ing of watch-spring crinolines there against, every
time we walk with the adored one of our heart
down Regent Street. We feel *that*, don't we ?
And when we are stifled in omnibuses, or hustled
out of our stall at the theatre, or put to the *peine
forte et dure* at dinner-tables, the inconvenience
we suffer becomes to a certain extent palpable
and tangible. Not long ago, in the wilds of
Yorkshire, I went to church one Sunday morning with a charming family of young ladies, of
whose worthy papa I was the unworthy guest.
(Please not to insert this in the "New York
Eavesdropper," to the intent of my being brand-

ed six months afterwards, in the columns of the
" Asafœtida Review," as a dastardly betrayer of
the secrets of the Lares and Penates.) The
church was open, you see, to everybody, although
I went in the family-pew ; and ninety-nine hun-
dredths of the females among the congregation
wore crinoline. A nice time I had of it. My
four fellow-worshippers made as many " cheeses "
of crinoline around me. There was no way out
of it. Oh, for Lord Ebury to have shortened
this one particular morning service ! There was
so much distended whalebone about me, that I
felt myself off the coast of Greenland ; a mere
tub, thrown out for young whales. I couldn't
move ; I couldn't feel my hassock or my pocket-
handkerchief. It was a continual uprising and
down-plumping of crinoline. I was a miserable
man. The sermon was an excellent one ; but I
couldn't hear it. The singing was unusually
good, for a country church ; but it grated on my
ears. I shall never forget the agony of that experience of the Litany under the influence of exaggerated crinoline. I could enlarge on my
woes ; but desist, for fear of being Spurgeon-
esque. Hircius, who is most orthodox, and was
a church-rate martyr in 1836, just before he was
bankrupt in the corn-and-coal line, would be
shocked at my profanity ; and Spungius, who
married a pew-opener when the secularist cheese-

monger's widow had thrown him over, would never forgive me.

But, granting the aches and pains, pecuniary and personal, which may afflict the descendants of Adam through the addictedness to preposterous skirts of the daughters of Eve, I say boldly that the old garments of the ladies were quite as productive of mental and physical discomforts to us and to themselves. How about the frocks of 1830, worn high up above the ankles? How about the monstrous ladies' hats, that knocked our own off, and took up all the room inside the Brighton "Highflyer?" Discourse unto me, I, pray thee, concerning those hideous bishop and leg-o'-mutton sleeves, forever flapped on our faces, or dabbled in the gravy at dinner. Conjure up again the shawls you were always called upon to pin behind, the sandal shoe-strings that were always becoming untied; to say nothing—well, there can be no harm in mentioning it.

Every gentleman whose wife has not kept a lady's maid has been called upon, in the old time, to lace a lady's corset. In Haydn's song a young lady is desired by her mamma to "lace her boddice blue" herself; but in married life Benedict used to be, with perfect propriety, called upon to perform that cheerful office. I say, used to be; for the days of stay-tyranny are happily gone by. Many ladies have abandoned the use of corsets altogether; while, for those who still adhere to these adjuncts to feminine symmetry, cunning Parisian *corsetières* have devised on anatomico-physiologico-hygienic principles, natty little structures, of elastic nature, which are hooked-and-eyed, or buttoned or strapped, and slipped on and off, with the extremest comfort and despatch. Benedict is not called upon to lace Beatrice's stays now. Let us be joyful. Young English ladies used to kill themselves in the attempt to have wasp-waists. Dreadful stories used to be told of English mothers forcing their daughters to wear suffocating, chest-compressing, rib-crushing stays, by night and by day, or strapping them up to the bedpost, to get a better purchase while they laced them. And how hideous, after all, were the hour-glass bodices, the wasp-waists? A very famous English artist made the other day, I am told, *par fantaisie*, a drawing of the Venus de Medicis as she stands in Florence—" to enchant the world "—and the Venus in stays and crinoline. Under the last-named aspect she looked frightful. Hogarth tried an analogous experiment in one of his prints; and you may see a Venus in a hoop in the background of the picture of " Modern Polite Conversation."

Every schoolgirl knows that the rage for hoops, *paniers*, or *marquises*, as they were distinctly called, was quite as fierce a century and a half ago as in our own time. The ladies' brocaded sacks were quite as ample, if not ampler, than our own *moire antiques*.

But just dwell for a moment on the very long duration of the huge-skirt mode. Hoops in some form or another lasted from the time of Queen Anne to the middle of the reign of George the Third—for at least seventy years. And don't suppose that crinoline in good Queen Anne's time was quite a new thing. The portraits of Titian and Parmegiano show that the dames of the middle ages understood to its very base the secret of exuberant skirts. Look at Zucchero's picture of Queen Elizabeth, and consider the kirtles and farthingales of her maids-of-honor, all stuffed and bombasted out with silk and wadding. Crinoline in some guise or another will endure, I am afraid, for years after I have been measured for my last surtout—elm, plain, richly studded with japanned nails—and skirts will be worn *à la*— Halloa! what's that? Silence that dreadful bell! I know it too well; and the dubious female party with the mysterious parcel (shaped and pinned as no other parcel on earth is pinned and shaped), who glides upstairs and looks at me askance, as a creature to be loathed and scorned until it is time for him to pay a certain little bill. Thank goodness, I am safe in Bed, and at Breakfast-time she cannot blight me with her baleful glances. Skirts are worn *à la* Ruination; and that confounded ring at the bell must be from Somebody's Dressmaker. .

ON THE CONDITION OF MY POOR FEET.

"JOSEPH," once said a wise man, who had just been utterly ruined and overthrown in the battle of life, to his attached man-servant, "I am going to bed. You will give me, if you please, forty drops of laudanum on a lump of sugar, and you will wake me up the day after to-morrow. After that we will see what can be done."

There is nothing like going to bed under trying circumstances, and stopping there. If nature has not endowed you with a somnolent faculty—if you don't, to your misfortune, belong to the great order of sleepy-heads—you had best take the laudanum on the lump of sugar, as per recipe foregoing. But I earnestly recommend you to sleep upon it. Stay in bed as long as ever you can. The world must go round; and perhaps your affairs, having come to the worst, may take a turn with it. If you wake, turn over on to t'other side, and go to sleep again and again, until you find yourself so hungry that you must needs leap out of bed and proceed to devour something or somebody. That same great order of sleepy-heads, to whom I have just alluded, are,

after all, the people who get on best in the world.
They don't "fash" themselves. They fret not
themselves because of the ungodly. They just
pull their night-caps over their brows, shut their
eyes, find out the cosiest corner in the undula-
tions of the pillow, and take forty times, or forty
thousand times, forty winks; and at their uprising the odds are forty to one that, desperate as
things seemed when they fell a-snoozing, they
have now mended. Cæsar—J. Cæsar of Rome,
as poor crazy Mr. Train used to call that con-
queror—desired to have men about him that
were fat, *and such as slept o'nights.* He liked
not yon Cassius, who had a " lean and hungry "
—and a wakeful look, you may be sure. Do you
think Lord Palmerston would remain, at seventy-
nine, our " ever versatile, vivacious, and juvenile
Premier," if he didn't fold his arms, tilt his hat
on to the tip of his nose, tuck his legs under the
Treasury Bench, and go comfortably to sleep
while the bores of the Opposition were prosing,
and Caucasian serpents biting the file? He wakes
up when the cistern of disparagement has finished plapping, and comes up smiling, and de-
molishes his antagonists all round. There are
people who habitually go to sleep in omnibuses,
and on suburban railways; but I never knew
them to miss their station, or to fail in proguing
the conductor in the ribs at the right moment.

There are worshippers who make a point of going
to sleep in church, be the sermon dullest or the
most exciting of discourses; yet they always
know the text, and are reckoned great judges of
orthodoxy. There are people who go to sleep at
the theatre, waking up only at the conclusion of
each act; yet I have frequently had occasion to
admire the terseness and acumen with which
they criticise the piece. And if you will only
be good enough to go to sleep over the opening
paragraph of this present number of Breakfast in
Bed, and, waking at the end, declare it to be the
best of the series, I shall have the very highest
respect for your taste and discrimination, and
shall be eternally grateful to you.

I say to you, then, sleep upon it! Good-night,
Signor Pantaloon; you will be all the better for
your nap the day after to-morrow morning. If
Victorine hadn't slept upon it, all the woes she
dreamt of might have been realised in actual life.
" Sleep, gentle lady !"—slumber is good for your
complexion, your nerves, and your temper; good,
also, it may be, for the peace of mind of the
harassed helot, Man. Remember those prudent
young men of Ephesus during the dark ages.
They had the sagacity to discern that there was
no use in making head against the prevailing
persecution of the Christians : that they would
take nothing by their motion in being martyrised.

What did they do? They betook themselves to a comfortable cave, went to sleep, slept for centuries, and woke up with a tremendous appetite for their Breakfast in Bed, and to find that the world had become converted to the Christian faith.

I have always thought that Napoleon would have acted wisely in going to sleep for a couple of days or so after his defeat at Waterloo. Something advantageous to Imperialism might have turned up in the interim. Instead of indulging in a tranquil doze twice or thrice round the clock, the restless adventurer must needs go fuming about the Elysée, and chopping logic with Benjamin Constant, and playing at cross-purposes with the Senate and the Legislative Body (who, being Frenchmen, were, of course, intriguing for the destruction of him whom they deemed abandoned by Fortune); and then Lord Vilainton, and Field-Marshal Blucher, and Schwarzenburg, and Barclay de Tolly, and the whole horde of the Allies, came up, and there was an end to Napoleon the Great, who thenceforth was privileged to sleep as much as ever he liked at St. Helena —a dreary siesta, which had no waking but in a miserable death.

Some people—ministers of state and others— forbid their servants to wake them if good news arrive while they are asleep. They only desire to be aroused if disastrous tidings come. I say, sleep on, through good and through evil report. Let the good get better, and the bad right itself, if it can. Nowhere is the philosophy of this doctrine more forcibly illustrated than in the history of Mr. Moss Abrahams and Mr. Isaac Solomonson.

Mr. Moss Abrahams had accepted a bill of exchange, of which Mr. Isaac Solomonson was the holder. Late on the eve of the acceptance coming due, Mr. Abrahams discovered that he was destitute of funds wherewith to meet it. Being a conscientious and withal a nervous man, he forthwith hies him to Mr. Solomonson's residence. It was midnight, and the holder of the bill had long since (like a wise man of business) retired to rest. But Mr. Abrahams was determined to inform him of his impecuniosity, and knocked him up.

After a little while his creditor put his nightcapped head out of the second-floor window, and demanded, with some asperity, who was there.

" It ish I, Mr. Isaac Sholomonson," responded Mr. Moss Abrahams.

" And vot do you vant, Mr. Mosh Abrahams, at thish time of nightsh?" pettishly asked Mr. Solomonson.

"O Mr. Isaac Sholomonson, O Mr. Isaac Sholomonson!" quoth the disconsolate accepter;

"you must be told the newsh. There is a billsh for forty-shcven pound ten due to-morrow, and I cannot pay it. I cannot shleep for thinking of it, Mr. Sholomonson."

"Go to the devilsh!" cried out Mr. Isaac Solomonson, in a rage; "go to the devilsh, Mr. Mosh Abrahams! *It is I who cannot shleep, since you cannot pay the billsh!*"

With which he banged down the window, and sued the defaulter next day, dreadfully.

Imprudent Abrahams! if he had gone to bed, and allowed Mr. Solomonson to slumber undisturbed, that last-named worthy might have woke next day in a good temper, and given his debtor time.

All these are capital theories—is it not so?—but, like fine words, they butter no parsnips. How about reducing them to practice? Here am I, for instance, tumbling and tossing on the uneasy couch to which I retired at one o'clock this morning; and I can obtain no rest. This is Wednesday, the eighteenth day of March. Since Friday night the sixth, I have had, perhaps, about one-seventeenth part of the natural rest without which, the doctors tell, and nature warns us, human beings are apt to go raving mad. I have been to bed over and over again. I have carried my slumberousness about with me, as Christian, in Bunyan's allegory, did his burden of sins; but

I cannot depose that grim fardel. Leaden weights hang to mine eyelids; but they refuse to recognise the laws of gravity, and quiescence will not shake them off. I can sleep a little standing; but refreshing slumbers desert me when I lie down. I can doze in cabs and railway-carriages; but in bed I am horribly wakeful. I think it would do me good if I went to sleep for a fortnight. I seem to have been in bed for six months, but no good has yet come of it. My Breakfast lies untasted before me, and half a dozen times I have all but kicked the tray off the bed. I am the Weasel; but, oh, how grateful I should be if somebody could only just catch me napping, and shave my eye-brows off.

I know what it is this time; I know what prevents me obtaining even the eight hours' bare rest which are said to be requisite for a Fool! O my kind friends! it isn't a question of liver; it isn't pancreas; it isn't devilled kidneys; it isn't pork-chops for supper; it isn't that other glass of Moselle—I have subsisted chiefly on blotting-paper, quill-pens, and abernethy-biscuits these ten days past; it isn't conscience—I haven't robbed a church, or murdered one of my blood-relations; since Wednesday week I have stolen nothing but precious days from my life; I have defrauded nobody but Nature; I have murdered nothing but the Queen's English. What is it,

then, that makes my bed a rack, and my counterpane red-hot coals, and my breakfast loathsome, and myself intolerable to me? It is the
condition of my Poor Feet.

Well, I suppose there is nothing immodest (even
in this wonderfully nice-spoken age) in confessing
that I am afflicted with corns, defying the most
recondite efforts of pedicurism. Hannah More
was troubled, I have been given to understand,
with bunions—and yet she was a good woman.
The greatest statesmen in this constitutional country have suffered from the gout. If it be a crime
to be hereditarily podagrous, take me to the
Tower and clap me into the bilboes at once.
Then, again, as to varicose veins. Is a man irre-
trievably ruined, in a moral sense, if he be subject to that last-named ailment? If such be the
case, put me down as a lost one. Finally, there
is such a condition of frame known in the language
of the vulgar as being "weak on the pins." I
am feeble on the supporters. I don't like walking. When I do pedestrianise, my unlucky legs
are always carrying me to the wrong places, and
wretchedness and misfortune congregate like
shards and pebbles beneath my poor feet.

Within the last few days I have been asked at
least a thousand times how those poor feet were.
The interrogation would not have troubled me
had it been put in a kindly, in a sympathizing

spirit, and by people I knew; but how would you like a screeching multitude, fifty thousand strong, and with not one of whom, to the best of your knowledge, you had even a bowing acquaintance, to vociferate in your track—in the public street, mind—" Ya-a-a-h! how are your poor feet?" *I* know how my poor feet are by this time. My brothers, they are swollen to the size and consistency of pumpkins. I feel that I shall never be able to put them to the ground again. Henceforth I must go abroad in a bowl, like a *cul de jatte*, or on a trolly, with a pair of leaden dumps to steady myself, or in a go-cart, or in a sedan-chair.

My poor feet have been stamped and trodden upon by innumerable feet. The hoofs of Her Majesty's Household Cavalry have passed over me. Those hoofs have made painful indentations on the softest parts of my anatomy. I have been kicked and beaten; I have been knocked down and trampled upon; I have been rolled into the gutter; I have been charged by the Royal Horse Artillery; I have been under the carriage-wheels of the Corporation of London. The metropolitan police have assaulted me; eighteen times have I been garotted by the hands of authority gone out of its mind. I am one bruise. Ecchymosis and I are synonymous.

Stop! my poor feet are *not* quite so large as

pumpkins. There must be exaggeration in such a simile. But can you imagine the condition of a wretched Egyptian fellah who has just had an interview with the Cadi, and who, according to the pugnant expression of Eastern penal jurisprudence, has just "eaten stick" for non-payment of taxes, that is to say, has undergone the agony of the bastinado, till the soles of his feet are reduced to pulp? I have read in the book of a French tourist, how, after one of these banquets of stick, the miserable victim of fiscal ruthlessness has crawled out of the Hall of Justice on his hands and knees, grovelling and wallowing his way along, till, reaching the outside of the court, his pitying relatives have enveloped his poor feet in vine-leaves smeared with olive-oil, and swathed them in linen bandages, and borne him home, moaning, on their shoulders.

To such a state do my poor feet approximate; yet wretcheder I than the Egyptian, or "any other fellah," for I had nobody to carry me home, and the cabs on Saturday night refused to budge under five shillings a mile. There wasn't a Ryal Hentry hevery day in the year, they said.

The manner of its coming about—of my poor feet being gelatinized, I mean—was this. Yielding to the representations of some very good friends of mine, who, with infinite pleasure to the public, and great profit to themselves, conduct a daily newspaper of large circulation, I consented for some twenty-four hours to abdicate the honorable position of a rent-and-tax paying English gentleman, and to become a penny-a-liner. Now there is nothing intrinsically despicable in the status of the meritorious and useful individuals whose more courteous designation is that of " occasional reporters," and who furnish graphic, and in the main truthful, narratives of fires, murders, accidents, and Lord-Mayor shows, for a certain sum of copper, per line, for publication in the columns of the metropolitan press. These chroniclers, whether they be paid at the rate of a penny, or three-halfpence, or twopence-halfpenny a line, form an exceedingly industrious, inoffensive, and intelligent class, and are often much better worth their salt than more pretentious scribblers—I name no names—who are remunerated for their lucubrations at the rate of five guineas a page. But the gluttonous, bibulous, inconstant, ungrateful British public have taken it into their conceited heads that an occasional reporter is necessarily a ragged creature, with a soiled note-book, a battered hat, and a bulging umbrella ; a kind of cross between Paul Pry, a detective policeman, and a man in possession ; that he is poor and miserable, as well as humble and obscure ; and that it is therefore expedient to laugh at and to despise him.

Only the other day, travelling by the South-Western Railway, I overheared a gross, muddle-headed, City kind of man, swelling with an over-weening sense of his own importance, criticising the account of the marriage of the Prince of Wales, which had appeared that morning in the "Times" newspaper.

"What stuff these penny-a-liners do write to be sure!" quoth my gross *vis-à-vis* to his neighbor. It would have been as much probably as either of them could do in the literary line to have written "cash, Dr.; contra, Cr.," at the head of a ledger, having reference to transactions in cheese or black-lead. The "penny-a-liners" whose "stuff" excited their ineffable spleen, happened to have been, on the one part, a gentleman who was "the Pen of the War" throughout the Crimean campaign, during the Indian Mutiny, and in the early and most momentous episodes of the American struggle. On the banner of William Howard Russell (who was in the nave of St. George's Chapel at the Prince's marriage) are emblazoned the words "Sebastopol," "Cawnpore," and "Potomac." His comrade, Mr. Nicholas Woods (who was in the gallery overlooking the choir), is, although younger, as familiar as he with battles and

shipwrecks, with peril, with hardship, and with
disease. These men have gone through all that
the most approved warriors can endure. They
have confronted death in every shape; they
have made famous the achievements of their
countrymen all over the world; and, in conso-
nance with an agreeable and highly practical
code of Social Law, not a star glitters on their
breasts, not a whisper of their names is made in
a despatch or a gazette; and their sole reward—
beyond the applause of the select few who know
their worth—is to be called "penny-a-liners"
by a fat, ignorant cheesemonger; ay, and the
taunt can be as glibly and impudently and men-
daciously repeated by thousands who are neither
fat, nor ignorant, nor cheesemongers.

Well, I took up my pilgrim's staff and scrip
cheerfully, and I agreed, as a "penny-a-liner,"
in the caseous acceptation of the term, to write
an account of the entry of the Princess Alexandra into London. I was to take the procession
up at London Bridge, and to follow its course as
far as Pall Mall; and as I did not happen to be
capable, like Sir Boyle Roche's bird, of being in
two places at once, and furthermore, as, by
remaining stationary either at the Bridge, or
at the Mansion House, or at a window in
Cheapside, or in the gallery at St. Paul's, or
in Fleet Street, or the Strand, or Trafalgar

Square, I could have seen the pageant only as a passing vision, and should have missed its most astonishing framework, the crowd—it was ̖ arranged that I should follow in its wake along the streets from the confines of the City to the West End. How to do so without let or hindrance was a ˙ chief object of solicitude. The police along the line of route were first to be thought of by one who didn't wish to be knocked down or taken into custody for intruding himself where he had no business to be.

I conceived that, in the interest of the public, who would be crazy to read a complete account of the royal entry in the newspapers on Monday morning, I had more than a right—I had an absolute call—to see as much of the procession as I possibly could. So I addressed myself to Captain Hodgson, the acting Commissioner of the City Police, and obtained from that courteous but overworked functionary a buff card, empowering "bearer to pass along the line on foot." A similar card, but white in hue, had been procured for me from the Commissioner of Metropolitan Police ; but wishing to make assurance doubly sure, I wrote on Friday afternoon a pretty litle *poulet* to Sir Richard Mayne, at his bower by Whitehall, stating who I was, the nature of the essentially public service I had undertaken to perform, the need there was for persons representing the daily newspapers to be permitted to circulate unimpeded from point to point, and sundry little *gentillesses* of that description.

Sir Richard Mayne, K.C.B., sent me, by the commissionnaire attached to the club of which I am a humble member, his compliments and another card, with, "To the police along the line. Pass the bearer on foot.—Richard Mayne;" the pasteboard stamped with the royal arms, and the whole enclosed in the handsomest official envelope it has ever been my privilege to gaze upon. "Come," I said, with premature complacency, "who shall accuse *les gens de la police* of want of courtesy after this?" Alas, I little knew what was to happen to my poor feet!

I was up the next morning by seven, prepared for a leisurely promenade along the streets, well-lined and kept by policemen, soldiers, and volunteers, from the Bricklayers' Arms to Paddington. Suddenly there arrived a missive from a friend, who had likewise accepted the mission of a penny-a-liner. "The Corporation of London," he wrote, "have permitted the representatives of the press to follow the civic procession in an open carriage. There is a place reserved for you in a landau, which will convey you as far as Temple Bar; after that (the civic *cortége* filing up Chancery Lane) you must shift for yourself. Moreover, the Lord

Mayor and the Reception Committee will be happy to see you to breakfast at Guildhall, at half-past ten o'clock precisely."

Need I say that I didn't Breakfast in Bed on the morning of Saturday, the 7th of March? I like breakfasting with Corporations. It makes you, for the time, feel wealthy and substantial. My friend with the landau happened to be a neighbor; so blithely I trudged from the Square of Russell to the Square of Brunswick, and at the portal of one of the mansions therein, I found the carriage, "drawn by two noble steeds." It was like going to the Derby, only the hamper was to be found by the Fathers of the City. We started about nine, with a full complement of ladies, children, and gentlemen. The former we were to drop in divers localities in the City, whence the procession could be witnessed. The founder of the feast—I mean of the landau—left us in King William Street, being bound for Gravesend, where he was to witness the disembarkation of the Princess.

Even at this early period of the morning the streets were almost impassable, and it was a quarter past ten ere we reached the entrance to Guildhall Yard. In Guildhall I found three gentlemen who were to be my companions in the famous landau: one was an eloquent and deservedly popular London clergyman; the second

7

was a dramatist and essayist of repute ; the third
was a barrister, writer of leading articles, and
habitué of the Reporters' Gallery in the House of
Commons. Nay, the landau was to hold five.
Place number four was to be occupied by a
gentleman from the " Times ;" and the fifth personage in the triumphant chariot was to be the
hapless orphan with the poor feet who has now
the melancholy pleasure to address you. For the
nonce we were all penny-a-liners. Briefly will
I dismiss the breakfast in Guildhall, albeit it was
the only event throughout the day that was un-
mingled with agony.

The Corporation comported themselves, as
they always do, with hospitality and politeness.
They gave me a hearty welcome, and a bridal
favor as big as a pancake. I might have feasted
upon game-pie, *foie gras*, cold turkey, Moselle,
blanc-mange, and other delicacies, had they not
all entered into the grim Index Expurgatorius of
my medical attendant. But everything looked
rosy-colored: Aldermen in cocked hats; Common Councilmen in furred gowns; the City Mar-
shal as large as life; the ward-beadles with their
gilt pokers; the Lord Mayor's state footmen; the
deputy-lieutenants in their scarlet and silver. All
this, combined with hand-shaking, snuff-taking,
the pinning-on of favors, and the popping of
champagne-corks, conduced to a feeling of exhila-

ration easier to be imagined than described. You
see that I have adopted, with cheerful alacrity,
the penny-a-liner's style.

We didn't get on very well with our landau.
We found it waiting for us at the bottom of
Aldermanbury, after breakfast; but as it happened to be at the precise tail-end of the procession, and there were some hundreds more open
carriages before us, all crammed with dignitaries
of the Corporation and the City guilds, and all
jammed up, apparently inextricably, in a com-
pact mass, the chance of our getting to London
Bridge, or to the Mansion House, or to Cheapside,
or to anywhere else on this side Ultima Thule,
became, by one o'clock in the afternoon, exceed-
ing shady, not to say hopeless. We—the clergyman, the barrister, the dramatist, and the "Times"
man—bore it as long as we could ; but when the
probability of the Princess's having arrived, having passed through Temple Bar, and being full
trot on her way to Paddington, assumed more
and more tangible proportions, we began to grow
nervous for the welfare of the public, of our proprietors and ourselves. First we made jests about
the immovable landau ; then we grumbled at
its immobility ; then we devoted it wholesale to
perdition.

Finally we abandoned it to its fate ; and
telling the coachman to pick us up wherever he

could find us in the line of procession, we made
our way to Guildhall again, pushing, grinding,
and jostling through the well-packed throng, and
found the head of the civic train just about
moving.

It was one of the most inconceivable jumbles
of brass-bands, rifle volunteers, policemen on
horseback and policemen on foot, horse-artillery-
men, aldermen, common councilmen, javelin-men,
watermen, standard-bearers, ticket-porters, and
long-shore men, that was ever visible out of the
phantasmagoric vision of a raving maniac, with
superadded *delirium tremens*, who has been
supping on raw pork-chops with Mr. Home the
medium, and reading Hoffmann's Tales, and the
" Woman in White " to the accompaniment of
cavendish tobacco and strong green tea. My
poor feet began to suffer. Once or twice I was
lifted off them bodily, and then asked in indignant terms, " vere I vos a shovin' to ?" I shoved
at last into the midst of a group of ancient persons clad in red-baize jerkins, with pewter
platters on the breasts thereof, jockey-caps, knee-
smalls, and white stockings, with ankle-jacks à la
" Roberto Pulveroso," or " Dusty Bob." These
strange and weird creatures all carried banners
covered with heraldic emblazonments of anti·
quated aspect. On inquiry, I found one of them
to contain the arms of the " late Sheriff Cow-

dery." Who was Cowdery, and when did he die?

Another bore the cognizance of "the late Countess of Kent." Why, bless me! that must have been Joan, the fair countess, who married Edward the Black Prince! That comely widow has been dead something considerably over five hundred years.

These venerable standard-bearers seemed to belong to another world. In two points only could they claim affinity to the present century. Knee-breeches, cotton stockings, and ankle-jacks, for the first, were not habitually worn in the Middle Ages; and for the second, these weird servitors all smelt strongly of rum, a spirit which was hardly popular as a stimulant in this country previous to the colonization of the West Indies.

However, in a common crush we are all equal. Clergyman, barrister, dramatist, journalist, and standard-bearers—we all trudged on, a band of brothers.

Nay, there even affiliated himself unto us a gentleman in corduroy, much japanned with grease, and wearing the shockingest hat I have gazed upon for many a day. He smelt even more powerfully of rum than the ancient standard-bearers, to one of whom he stood in the relation of brother-in-law, or of bosom friend, or of

" mate," though out of civic costume. When his friend was tired, he carried his banner for him —indeed I did as much for another weazened old mortal in red baize; but he was careless as to how he carried it; and he flapped the silk in my eyes, and occasionally stood the pole at ease on my poor feet with the utmost *insouciance*.

He was moreover quarrelsome in demeanor, unsteady in his gait, and decidedly not choice in his language. On the whole, I hope to be dispensed, for some time to come, from the companionship of such a drunken, abusive vagabond as the gentleman in corduroy proved himself to be.

My agonies continued literally from morn to dewy eve, for it rained cats and dogs before six P.M. How I managed to squeeze on to London Bridge, and, when the Prince and Princess had passed, to squeeze off it again ; how I was jostled through the City, and fairly knocked down at Temple Bar, ground against the walls of that structure, and galloped over by a squadron of Dragoons ; how the Metropolitan Police exhibited an utter indifference to Sir Richard Mayne's passport, and vehemently informed me that I should *not* pass along the line on foot— whereupon I as vehemently declared that I must and would pass, and dared them to take me into custody, and defied them to mortal combat—which physically I got lamentably the

worst of, but was morally victorious, for I
gained my end, and got from Temple Bar to
Pall Mall, five minutes after the royal carriage
had passed ; how at last, bruised, bleeding, ex-
hausted, and blacker than any sweep, I saw, in
the gallery erected in front of a certain pala-
tial edifice in Pall Mall, the bonnet of the wife
of my bosom ; how, my out-of-door task being
over, I mentally bade the royal procession go
hang, and with a last desperate plunge through
the mob, reached the steps of the Club, and pro-
cured lobster-salad and the sparkling vintage of
Epernay for the wearer of the bonnet and her
companion ; how I gnawed the leg of a fowl with
a grim sense of complacency at sitting at last
under my own fig-tree, with no man to make me
afraid—not even the dunderheaded police, and
the remarkably obtuse and discourteous Captain
Labalmondiere, who seemed to think that Sir
Richard Mayne had granted passes to the representatives of the press as a mere joke, and was for
driving me back from Trafalgar Square eastward,
but was baffled by my persistence and agility ;
how we couldn't get a cab home, and nobody
would lend me a brougham, and I had lent my
own to " a lady friend " (which her name is Harris) ; how the new bonnet was spoilt in the rain,
and we reached home about eight ; and how,
after drinking about a gallon and a half of tea, I

sat down to work, and wrote all that night and the best part of the next day (breaking the Sabbath, alas!), in order that the British public might read all about the reception of the Prince and Princess in the newspapers on Monday morning;—all these things are written in other chronicles, and it boots not now to dwell upon them with more particularity. I drank, let it suffice to say, the cup of penny-a-lining to the very last dregs.

But was it not all my own doing? I had laid down the mantle of respectability, and taken up the toga of the penny-a-liner. I was nobody—less than nobody. The crowd knew it, and laughed my nothingness to scorn. Five thousand "roughs" pointed me out with the dirty finger of derision, and five thousand City Arabs howled at me. It is my custom to dress in black—being generally in mourning for my relatives, or my friends, or myself; and nature, not unassisted by art, has conferred upon me a red nose. The crowd in Cheapside declared that I was a mute. They called me bone-grubber. They assailed me with much more invective, coupled with many more expletives, which I disdain to transcribe. It was all my own fault. What business had I with "occasional reporting?"

My friends have been telling me so ever

since. I have derogated, they inform me, from my standing in letters and in society. I answer, that I have no such pediment left—only a pair of poor feet, which I can't stand upon; that I voluntarily accepted a duty; that I carried it out to the best of my ability; and that I haven't a single toe-nail left.

ON A REMARKABLE DOG.

FROM the lower regions of this establishment comes wafted towards me, in rippling freshets of sound, softened and mellowed by divagation, a deep baying. With the utmost regularity every morning, while I am Breakfasting in Bed, just as I have begun to crunch my second slice of dry toast, I hear that baying. There is no mistaking its import. I know what it means, quite as well as I do the signification of the knocks and rings at the door about this time in the morning. For example, there is the milk, with her customary *ranz des vaches*—a vaccine arrangement which, I much fear, has been associated, since we have been resident in London, with the handle of the pump nearest to the dairy where the professedly lacteal fluid is concocted for metropolitan consumption. Then there is the baker, whose knock is a determined one, and who is an individual of arrogant mien, but who has been slightly less independent since the carts of the Aërated Bread Company (Limited) took to calling for orders. Between the milk and the baker, the watercress-seller makes himself audible at the area-railing,

and directly afterwards the first intonation of
" Clo' !" is heard from the street.

If I draw aside the window-blind a little, and
peep, I am pretty sure to see the Hebrew gentleman from Houndsditch glancing wistfully upwards, as though in meek remonstrance at the
closed casement of my bower. " Why does that
lazy fellow persist in Breakfasting in Bed? why
doesn't he come down, like a man, and sell me
three pairs of old trousers and a little veskit?"—
I fancy the harmless Caucasian is murmuring.

Then the postman's knock, in its sharp, impe-
rious rat-tat, makes you start and shudder. I
believe it was Mr. Howard Glover who, in con-
junction with an artist in chromo-lithography,
undertook to inculcate the extremely erroneous
theory that everybody was glad to hear the postman's knock. I would give the functionary in
question a very long holiday, had I the power of
dismissal. I never knew any good that came out
of the General Post-Office—nay, nor out of the
defunct twopenny institution. Next to the agony
of writing letters must rank, I think, the torture
of receiving them; yet, personally, I am consoled
at the thought, that on one morning of the year
(Sundays always excepted) the postman leaves
my knocker alone. This solitary blissful occasion is Valentine's Day.

Let me see: is my reckoning according to

Cocker, and Colenso? The milk, the baker, the watercresses, the clothesman, the postman. Yes; I think they make up the sum of noises—the ordinary and distant street-cries, that don't concern you, being left out of calculation—till the newspaper-boy is due, and, with varying punctuality, makes his appearance. A young vagabond! The fibs that boy tells would have driven Baron Munchausen wild with envy. His mendacity is splendid in its boldness.

I am in the habit of taking in a high Tory morning journal, a rampantly Radical, a sententiously sentimental, and an icily Liberal one, and mixing up my perusal of them, paragraph for paragraph, in order to keep my head clear, and to cultivate a decent impartiality. In nine cases out of ten the newspaper-boy forgets, or omits, or refuses to bring one or another of the elements in this mental pabulum. The excuses he pleads are amazing in their variety and impudence: "They wos hall sold out at the hoffice;" "I couldn't get ne'er a copy no-how;" "The hother boy went hoff with five quire;" "Yourn was left at number heleven, round the corner;" "Missis is hill;" "Master won't let me have none;"—these are a few of his artful pleas in abatement; but his favorite one is, "The machine 'as broke down." It doesn't matter whether the non-forthcoming journal has a circulation of five hundred o of fifty thousand. The back of the "machine" is considered broad enough to bear any burden of blame, however onerous; and it has not unfrequently happened, that I have risen very early, or been kept up very late, and been at a newspaper-office and seen the ceremony of publication successfully completed, only to meet, on my return home, with the news-boy's cool assertion, that "The machine 'as broke down." He has very probably been playing fly-the-garter in the gutter, instead of waiting his turn at the office; or, if any momentous news have arrived, has sold the paper intended for me to a chance customer in the street, at a premium.

Hark! that baying sound is heard once more. If due attention be not paid to it, for the third time it will be audible, and in a remonstrant minatory tone; and then—though the .catastrophe happens but seldom—the house won't be large enough for the disturbance that will take place. There is no stopping one's ears to that baying. It is the voice of the dog BOODLEJACK demanding breakfast.

Voici la différence entre nous deux: Boodlejack has four legs, and I have two—it being granted, for the sake of argument, that I habitually walk erect. I sleep in the second-floor front, and Boodlejack in the back-yard. I Breakfast in Bed, Boodlejack in a kennel carpeted

with straw. Boodlejack bays for his breakfast, I
ring the bell for mine. If he doesn't get it as
quickly as he deems right and proper, he bays
again and again, and ultimately howls, barks,
rattles his chain, tears up his straw, kicks over
his water-pan, and overturns his kennel. If I
don't get my breakfast when I ring for it, I ring
again and again, and then—well, what do *you*
do, my revered friend, when your wishes are not
attended to? Do you bear your lot with angelic
patience, and after a lapse of half an hour falter
forth words of gratitude when somebody comes
up to ask whether you were pleased to ring or
not? or do you grumble, swear, kick off the bed-
clothes, give the servants warning, and threaten
to smash the furniture? As a middle course, I
should advise you to keep in your bed-room a
six-pound cannon-ball, or, better still, a pair of
dumb-bells.

If you experience any remissness of attention
to your summons, just open your bed-room door,
pop out on to the landing, and hurl the ball, or the
bells, with as much momentum as ever you can
muster, down-stairs. Those missiles will produce
so hideous and alarming a clatter in the house,
that, ere two minutes are over, the whole establishment will be on the *qui vive* at the door; and
then you may, with perfect ease and confidence
assume the angelic smile, and meekly hint that

you would feel very much obliged by a cup of tea being brought to you at the perfect convenience of the domestics. The suggestion of thus applying the useful metals to making one's wants known, I owe to the dog Boodlejack, who, when hard pushed for sustenance, is, as I have premised, given to rattling his chain against the wall of his kennel in a most horrifying manner.

I have noticed a few points wherein Boodlejack and I differ, albeit the difference is only one of degree; but there are many in which similarity between the dog and his master—if I *am* his master, physically or morally, the which I doubt sometimes—can be traced. Boodlejack has a temper; I have a temper. Boodlejack is gluttonous and lazy; I am ditto ditto. Boodlejack has a butcher; I have a butcher. I am allowed kidneys for breakfast twice a week; Boodlejack has tripe on Tuesdays and Fridays. For the rest, I hold Boodlejack to be quite as good as I am; although I very much doubt whether I am as good as Boodlejack.

In the garden of Newstead Abbey, Lord Byron erected, in the year 1808, a monument to a favorite Newfoundland dog named Boatswain. Towards this animal his lordship appears to have entertained something very like genuine affection; and the verses inscribed over his tombstone have sufficient cynicism, mingled with their

pathos, to make us believe in their sincerity.
The poetry is but so-so; for whenever a man has
to put sorrow into verse, his finer feelings are apt
to become absorbed in the exigence of tagging
rhymes together, and his muse begins to be redo-
lent of the shop, like a mute's countenance, or
the white pocket-handkerchief of a chief mourner.

> "When some proud son of man returns to earth,
> Unknown to glory, but upheld by birth,
> The sculptor's art exhausts the pomp of woe,
> And storied urn records who rests below."

This is very fine, but is bringing down the dog
at somewhat of a long shot. I like the prose
epitaph, still visible over Boatswain's grave, much
better.

> " Near this spot
> Are deposited the Remains of one
> Who possessed Beauty without Vanity,
> Strength without Insolence,
> Courage without Ferocity,
> And all the Virtues of Man without his Vices.
> This Praise, which would be unmeaning
> Flattery
> If inscribed over Human Ashes,
> Is but a just tribute to the Memory of
> BOATSWAIN, a Dog,
> Who was born at Newfoundland, May, 1803,
> And died at Newstead Abbey, November 18, 1808."

There is a fine healthy tone of misanthropy in

the line ascribing "all the virtues of man without his vices" to the poor defunct bow-wow,
almost smacking of the spirit which led Diderot
and Swift, in a congenial moment, to write books
against their own species. Swift, being mad,
published his—and the gorge of mankind will
continue, so long as letters last, to rise at the
loathsome picture of the Yahoos; but Diderot,
not being a crazy cathedral-dean and ex-counsel-
lor of the Tory ministry, but only an infidel
French encyclopedist, had sense enough to keep
his Satire upon Man in his own desk, and to burn
it before he died.

"All the virtues of man without his vices!"
The temper of the antithesis is charmingly characteristic. It is only when a man begins to find
out how bad he himself is that he discovers the
summum bonum to be resident in the lower animals. But are they "lower animals?" What
do I know of the mystery of the beasts? What
though the doctrine of the metempsychosis held
water, and Boodlejack were once upon a time a
bishop? He is greedy enough, and, with the assistance of the Tuesday and Friday's tripe, he is
growing fat enough for the episcopacy.

Now-a-days, when the principal functions of
Christian pastors seem to be confined to petition-
ing railway companies against running excursion
trains on Sundays, and orthodox Bishop A.'s

learning tails him, and compels him to resort to
the assistance of Layman B., to confute skeptical
Bishop C. on the vexed question of the hare
chewing the cud, and Noah's ark being big
enough to hold all the creeping things which,
according to Moses, went up into it—now-a-days,
when a bishop has grown, in the opinion of most
men, to be somewhat of the dummy or clothes-
prop kind of creature, I don't see why Boodlejack,
in an apron, and with a shovel-hat projecting
over his muzzle, should not write himself " Can-
tuar," or " Ebor," or " Dunelm." I question,
however—fond as he is of tripe, and partial to
whatever other " pretty tiny kickshaws," in the
way of bones, trimmings, and lumps of fat, the
cook may find him—whether his powers of de-
glutition are equal to eating up an income of
from five to fifteen thousand a year.

But let me leave for a time the Boodlejack
speculative for the Boodlejack absolute. First,
as to his name. Well, I will admit that is an
odd, perhaps an absurd one; but has not the proprietor of an animal the right to bestow whatever appellation he chooses upon his chattel? A
late eminent wit had two pigs, on which he conferred the cognomen of the publishers from
whom he derived the major part of his income.
Why shouldn't I call my dog Boodlejack, if I
elect so to do? The name may be ridiculous;

but, being devoid of meaning, is not liable to be resented as a personal affront by anybody. Suppose I had called him "Butler," or "Langiewicz," or "Two Hundred and Ninety," who knows what susceptibilities I might have wounded, what sensitive toes I might have trodden upon? There was never a human being, I opine, called Boodlejack, and I am therefore safe from any imputation of invidious motives. One is obliged to be so very cautious in these days, you see.

Besides, the dog's real name is not Boodlejack at all. Although it sounds like an amplification, it is *son petit nom*—his wheedling, caressing appellative. The brute's real name is Mungo. I named him Mungo the first hour he was brought to me, a black-nosed, liver-colored mastiff puppy, and a present from a young lady who is now gone to New Zealand. "Puppy," I said to him, as he grovelled, shivering and whining, on the hearthrug at my chambers in town, "your name is to be Mungo, as is fitting for such a sable-muzzled animal—and I shall expect you to behave yourself as such." He nearly worried my life out that morning. He was so very cold; and when you wrapped him up in a blanket, he essayed to swallow the corners, and nearly choked himself therewith.

Milk was brought to him; but he spurned it from him, and spilt it on the carpet. He would do nothing practicable, but climb over the fender and nestle among the coals. His little hide was pitted, ere long, with hot-coal marks ; but he had not sense enough to remove himself, or docility enough to suffer removal from the dangerous contiguity of the grate; and the burnt puppy did not dread the fire. The lady who had given him to me, was a young person of prompt decision and inflexible determination. When I tell you that, as a governess in Russia, she had kept a live bear in her sitting-room, you may imagine that she was not of the calibre to stand any nonsense. But I was powerless to do anything with the puppy. Although diminutive, he was savage. He bit me thrice before I had been acquainted with him as many half-hours, and his growl would have befitted a puppy four times his size. I lived then some twenty miles down the Great Western Railway ; and when it came to be time to catch the train, I borrowed a hand-basket and some flannel, crammed Mungo into it head fore-most, and took him away to Paddington.

When, after much growling and snapping, and very nearly compromising me with the railway company for surreptitious conveyance of animals in their carriages, I got him home, I did not say he had been presented to me by a young lady. I think I named a young gentleman, an old school-fellow, a friendly dog-fancier, or something of the

kind.   Life is so short, and so beset with inherent
woes, that it is best to avoid domestic disputes.
The secret was ere long divulged ; but it is, happily, a long way to New Zealand, and, as Mungo
speedily became beloved as the apple of the eye
by the head of the household, it mattered little
whether he was a present from Wirimu Kingi or
from Fair Rosamond.

But he did not remain Mungo, nor, indeed, a
mastiff puppy, long. He passed through the
transition stages of Mung, Bungy, Bumpy, Boo-
dle, and eventually became Boodlejack.   I grant
the etymological process to have been as recondite as that which derived " cucumber " from
King Jeremiah.   His change of breed was even
more remarkable.   He was about six weeks old
when I first knew him ; then he was all mastiff.
In his third month he looked uncommonly like a
bull-terrier.   Then he grew to the likeness of a
Newfoundland, only of the wrong color.   Then
his nose became elongated, his ribs defined, his
barrel prolonged, his haunches slendered, and he
resembled a greyhound.

At present, being about fifteen months old, I
am sure I don't know what he is like, save a very
big house-dog, with a terribly gruff voice, and an
insatiable appetite.   I have grown somewhat
chary of showing Mungo to my friends ; for I
used so to brag of him in his infancy as a suck-

ing mastiff, that, looking at him now, they burst into the guffaw of derision, and cry, "That a mastiff! why, he's nothing better than a mongrel!" Never mind what he is. He has the kindest and faithfullest heart that ever dog or man possessed ; and he is strong enough to tackle a garotter, and kill him.

At the house I took the liberty of occupying when Boodlejack, *alias* Mungo, was a puppy, there were four big dogs ; but they belonged, not to me, but to the landlord, and were placed on the premises quite as much for the purpose of protecting his own farm-yard, which adjoined our habitation, as for guarding us against the midnight marauder or the noonday tramp. You know that, chief among the delights of dwelling in a sequestered rural nook, is the apprehension, at almost every hour of the day and night, of being robbed. Our village, which was about three-quarters of a mile distant, was rather famous for housebreakers ; and I have no doubt that a neat little burglary to be committed in our house was "put up" about once a fortnight in one of the beershops of the adjacent hamlet. Our "crib," however, was never "cracked ;" and I am inclined to attribute our immunity from spoliation to the terrible renown for strength and ferocity of our four big dogs.

Not but if the blackguards who are in the

habit of making raids on country houses, with
shirts over their clothes, and crape over their
faces, and of murdering people in their beds if
they are disturbed in their enterprise, had possessed to the most limited extent the reasoning
faculty, they would have made very light of our
four dogs—leaving the infantile Boodlejack out
of the reckoning altogether—strong and valiant
as they were. In the first place, three out of
these four dogs were useless for any purpose of
giving an alarm ; for they howled and barked
all day and all night in the most persistent and
inconsequential manner. They cried " wolf"
when there was no wolf. They bayed the moon
and the night birds; they barked at the chickens
and the pigs ; they were driven to fury by the
barn-door cats ; and when they had nothing ani-
mate or inanimate to make a turmoil about, they
bewailed in dolorous accents their own hard fate
in being chained up, and having nothing to eat
but a bucket of gruel every morning, and the
hind-leg of a horse once a fortnight. The noise
they made was so continuous, that in the dead of
night even, we took no more notice of it than of
the screech-owls or the distant railway whistle.
The fourth dog was more serviceable. He was
a big bull, of a morose and secretive temperament.
He did not bark once in a month ; but when the
bull *did* give tongue, we all knew there was

something the matter, and rose from our beds
accordingly. Why not have let the dogs loose
at night? you may ask.

Not one landlord in a dozen dare do that. The
animals may be decoyed away, or poisoned by
prepared liver carefully distributed about the
bounds they are likely to beat. Moreover, I was
in the habit of returning by the last train from
London, which did not bring me to our village
till a quarter to one A.M.; and my landlord, who
dwelt in a little lodge close by, was even a later
bird than I. This is why we didn't let the dogs
loose.

The dog is a sagacious animal, the friend of
man, and very fond of his master in the day-
time; but at night his power of discriminating
between a burglar and an honest man is apt to
grow confused, and he is not unaddicted to pulling his proprietor down and tearing out his throat.
If the burglars had been logicians, they would
have bethought themselves of these things; but
happily they did not, and the renown of our four-
footed sentinels was quite sufficient to scare them
away.

Was it Boodlejack's fault if, educated on the
threshold of this turbulent guardroom, he grew
up to be somewhat rough, not to say fierce, in his
demeanor? He early, however, established a
claim to be considered a " remarkable dog " (else

I should have been ashamed to proclaim him as such at the head of this Paper), by drawing the nicest of distinctions between the people who were to be barked at and bitten, and those who were to be treated with courtesy and affection. Thus, he didn't bite me or mine, or the friends who were good enough (paying their own railway fare) to come and chop and sleep beneath my humble although picturesque roof-tree; but he flew at all tradespeople, as persons vending wares generally of inferior quality, and accustomed, besides, to call for sums of money which they alleged to be due to them at times and seasons not always convenient to his proprietors. Towards poor men, as a rule, he was pitiless. He hated the necessitous classes, the *bisognosos*, the importunate suppliants, with such a concentrated bitterness and remorseless activity, that you might have imagined him a relieving-officer, or a Government clerk.

The tramps and the Irishwomen who lurked about, under pretence of selling bobbins and muffatees and babies' caps, to see what they could lay their pilfering hands upon, he leapt up at savagely, and worried as well as his little teeth —oh, but they were sharp ones!—would allow him. To see him shake the corduroy, clay-caked leg of an agricultural vagrant would have done a Pharisee's heart good. He was so vindictive

towards small ragged children, that I had some
thoughts of re-christening him Malthus, deeming
him descended from some notable baby-tearer
erst in the possession of the reverend writer on
population. Blessings on the reverend writer's
pious memory ! and I hope he has got it hot by
this time. To the gipsies also he entertained the
liveliest aversion ; an aversion not uncommon
among those who reside in the arcadian districts,
and who do not habitually get their living by
begging or thieving. I am ashamed to say that .
I entertain not the smallest amount of sympathy
towards the Bohemian race.

A fellow-feeling does *not* make me wondrous
kind, or even commonly civil to them. Hircius
will be shocked to hear this. Spungius will lift
up his hands ; for is not my name Devil's-hoof?
Have I not lived under the blanket-roof, and
warmed the patched kettle with the farmer's
fagots to cook the poached hare? Have I not
found linen on every hedge? It may be so,
metaphorically ; but I would rather not have the
children of Egypt camping in my neighborhood.
I don't believe in their tinkering, and I don't
believe in their horse-whispering, and I don't
believe in their fortune-telling ; but I do believe
in their dirt, and their idleness, and their impudence, and their picking-and-stealing propensities.
Boodlejack was of my opinion, and was down on,

or rather up at the brownskins whenever they ventured within our gates.

It was another among the peculiarities of this remarkable dog, that he hated Eton boys. You are aware that, once seen, an Eton boy cannot be forgotten. Still less can he be confounded with any other boy belonging to any other school, academy, seminary, or collegiate institution whatsoever. He is about the prettiest, lithest, cleanest little lad you would wish to dwell upon. His hat is always shiny. It is always a chimney-pot hat. An Eton boy who wore a cap, or a pork-pie, or a wide-awake, would be, I suppose, after a birching *in terrorem* round the quadrangle, expelled the precincts of the antique spires. His lay-down collar is always snowy white. His trousers, his round jacket, his dandy scarf and waistcoat, are of faultless make. Nine out of ten Eton boys have gold watch-chains. Many, when out of bounds, have rings on their fingers. Few go to town without gloves. An Eton boy's hair is always well brushed. You can see in a moment that he belongs to the superior classes. And so, indeed, he does.

That fair-skinned urchin of eleven is the little Duke of Pampotter. He is heir to an estate of ninety thousand a year. He is a high and mighty prince. His father, the fifth duke (Claudius Polonius), was a Knight of the Garter; and some

of these days little Pampotter will have *his* stall
in St. George's chapel, and be written down K.G.
You can see at a glance that the boy is a gentleman. After all, there is something in Norman
blood, or at all events in illustrious descent.

Let me see, who is that other little urchin,
aged ten, who is accompanying his Grace into
the sweetstuff shop close to the Christopher?
He is quite as well dressed as the Duke. His
skin is as white. He is, on the whole, hand-
somer. Any Norman blood there, I wonder?
Not a bit of it. Urchin number two is Dickey
Brumstitch, and his father is an eminent army-
tailor and money-lender in Maddox Street, Han-
over Square. Give me a healthy baby, vaccinated
and so forth, and let me choose his nurses and
governesses, and direct his park-airings, and put
him to tutors, and send him to Eton, and I will
undertake to make a little duke out of a little
beggar's brat.

It is the diet, my dear sir, and the change of
air, and the pony exercise, and the fawning and
flattering that makes a gentleman, both for good
and evil, in the "Court-Guide" sense. For, give
me another baby, and let me poison his mother's
milk with bad air and scanty food. Let me rear
him in a Bethnal Green cellar, or give him a
Hoxton back slum to play about in. Let me
teach him to go to the gin-shop when he is four,

and to the pawnbroker's when he is six, and to
the Devil as soon afterwards as is convenient,
and I will go bail that my recipe is infallible for
manufacturing a young vagrant or a young
garotter out of a young descendant of the Planta-
genets.

But to return to the Eton boy in his connection with Boodlejack. His outward and visible
beauties I have already commented upon and
frankly admitted. As a rule, the Etonian is, besides, a good-natured, open-handed little fellow,
and about the worst-taught and worse-behaved
young cub to be discovered in any part of the
habitable globe. He is so because the system of
education under which he is bred is intrinsically
and hopelessly stupid, false, and rotten. A pack
of idiots, who know nothing about Eton schools
and Eton boys, go maundering about the world,
preaching up the " manly " and " independent "
qualities inseparable from the English public
school system. Manly and independent!

Do you know, madam, the first lesson taught
to your rosy-cheeked boy when he first goes to
Eton? It is to tell lies. His whole life out of
school is one course of shirking and evasion.
His masters forbid him to cross to the Berkshire
side of the bridge, or to be seen in a public-
house. He is continually lurking about the ta-
verns at Eton, or Windsor, or Salt Hill, with

some of his playmates as outlying scouts to watch
for the approach of a master.   As he grows bigger, his circle of prohibited pleasures widens.
The very men—clergymen of the Church of England—who are set over him to teach and train
him up in the way he should go, are perfectly
aware of the system of fraud and deception traditional in the school.   They even connive at it
by a tacit agreement, that if a boy be caught,
say, out of bounds, and takes to a hiding-place,
however flimsy—a sapling or a lamp-post, for instance—he shall be deemed to be concealed, and,
although visible as the sun at noon-day to the
master's eye, shall be held harmless from detec-
tion and punishment on his naked flesh.

Is this system at all a "manly and independent" one ?   Does it not the rather teach lads to
deceive their parents, their superiors, their friends
in after-life ?   He who has " chivied" from a master at Eton will not be very thick-skinned as
to "taking in the governor" about his college
and his regimental debts.   Of the "manly and
independent" elements to be found in flogging
and in fagging, I will only say thus much : that as
regards fagging, I was brought up in a school
where there were a thousand boys; that I went
into it a little boy and a weak boy ; and that if
any bigger boy had presumed, on his size or his
strength, to bully or to make a fag of me, I

would, failing redress from the school authorities, have gone out and bought a pistol, and blown the bully's brains out.

With respect to the maintenance in a professedly aristocratic school of a brutal and degrading punishment, which has been banished from parish-schools and workhouses, I have only to remark, that (as I suppose) whatever is, is right; and that if it be right that the basis of English aristocratic public-school education should be, for priests of the Christian religion to instil into little Christian boys an accurate knowledge of the beastly amours of heathen gods and goddesses by scourging their backs with birchen rods, I for one am not in the least astonished to find bishops of the same religion turning deists and blasphemers, and coming all the way from the Cape of Good Hope to tell us that the Noachian deluge is " unhistorical," and the Books of Moses nothing but supposes. It is all of a piece, and will be till lies cease to be respectable, and impostures cease to be institutions.

I am not inclined to think that my dog Boodlejack held views quite so uncompromising. He had not, probably, troubled his honest pate at all on the Etonian question. He had merely learnt from his doggish companions that, when Eton boys made their appearance about the farm, they were to be barked at, and if possible, bitten. I am not responsible for setting the initiative in this stern code.

My landlord had been an Eton boy himself; but he found a love for the antique spires incompatible with the preservation of peace and quietness on his farm. The young gentlemen from Eton were in the habit of coming across from the playing-fields and making playful raids on his property.

These blithe young moss-troopers would trample down his crops, play Old Gooseberry with his turnips, drive his cows half crazy by flicking them with twisted pocket-handkerchiefs, stone his ducks, chase his pigs, burst into his dairy, and romp with his dairy-maids. So, whenever he had a chance, he set the dogs upon them ; and when he hadn't, he would rush after them himself with a cart-whip, seize them in flagrant delict of trespass, and compel them to give up their names, which in good time were forwarded to Dr. Goodford, the head-master. I don't think he often took much by this part of his motion, as the boys—and small blame to them—usually trusted more to their imagination than to their memory for facts when interpellated.

A fine time this was for the dog Boodlejack. He had no fear of being held a trespasser, and might wag his tail, and come " flying all abroad," with his four legs very wide apart, over the best part of five hundred acres. He grew in size and beauty and strength, and was the admiration of all beholders; always excepting, I need scarcely say, the people he bit. The baker, for instance, didn't like him. He had had a triangular piece out of his leg. The laundress abhorred him. He had unlaced her boots for her and galled her heels many a time. But his most determined enemy was the village shoemaker. He was a shoemaker who undertook repairs; well, not to put too fine a point on it, he was a cobbler. A pair of boots of mine had been sent to this worthy Crispin to be mended, and he kept them twenty-seven days. It wasn't Easter-time; there was no fair or wake, fatal to sutorial industry, about. The household grew anxious, and Crazy Jane was despatched to Crispin to ask about my boots.

He pointed them out on a shelf, bright and natty, the perfection of cobblering.

" They've been done this fortnight," he said, moodily.

" Then why haven't you brought them back?" quoth Crazy Jane.

" Ain't they're a dawg up there at the Court?" asked Crispin, with darkling visage.

" Well, just a bit of a puppy," was the reply.

" A bit of a puppy !" Crispin repeated, with

8*

indignant scorn—" a roaring lion ! *I* know him.
He 'ave a bitten my Mariar Ann. He 'ave a
bitten my James. He 'ave anigh swallered up
my poor little black-and-tan tarrier Gyp, which
he did no more than pass the time of day to the
wicked, fearocious beast. He don't bite *me*.
'Ere's Mr. S.'s boots, and you may take 'em 'ome.
If you've brought the money, you may leave it;
and if you haven't, never mind about it, if it's
till next Christmas. I'll mend Mr. S.'s boots;
but I'm blowed if I'll come anigh that there ‾
dawg."

I believe the cobbler's bill for repairing my
boots has since been paid.

It was likewise about this time that Boodlejack, forgetful that his character of a Remarkable Dog entailed on him, morally, the responsibility of being a well-behaved one, began to
misconduct himself in the most distressing manner. Of his chasing ducks and chickens about
the farm-yard, and attaching himself in a friendly
but importunate manner to the tails of pigs, I am
not disposed to say anything very severe.. He
was yet but a puppy, and was full of his fun.
Nor was there, perhaps, anything to be bitterly
animadverted upon in his running down, garot-
ting, and slaying a rat very nearly as large as
himself, and which was so well known to the
denizens of our colony as to be called, from his

length and greyness of whisker, "Old Blucher," and was reported to be a hundred years old. This animal he dragged, after despatching it, to the lady of the house, and laid it at her feet as a peace-offering; and need of peace he had, indeed, when the numbers of reels of cotton he was in the habit of appropriating and essaying to devour every week of his life were taken into account.

But the conduct of Boodlejack speedily became more criminal. He grubbed up all the oval and diamond *parterres* in our garden. He made an *olla podrida* of all the seeds, and nasturtions came up where geraniums should have grown. We had a rosary, probably the prettiest and most prolific in the county of Bucks, and whose scented treasures were our delight and the envy of the whole country-side. Boodlejack cried havoc, and let loose the dogs of war—that is to say, himself—in the rosary. The brute's mouth was always full of rose-leaves, and he didn't seem to mind the thorns a bit. For so small a dog as he then was, you might have imagined, by the devastation he caused, that he was Atilla, king of the Huns. His frequent assaults on the legs of strangers made me fearful about the law. His predatory propensities were perilous.

He went out one day into the village with

Crazy Jane to buy some glazed calico. In Elder-
berry Lane whom should he meet but our curate's
wife with her little boy, the latter (aged three)
carrying a large home-made, open-work jam-tart,
newly presented to him by an admiring female
parishioner. The poor child had just begun to
revel in the delights of the tart, by smearing his
fingers with the jam, and dabbing his little digits
on his lips. There is an immensity of delecta-
tion to be had out of a jam-tart, if you only take
your time over it. The sight was too much for
Boodlejack. He bounced up to the curate's
little boy, frightened him out of his wits with
one piratical yelp, seized his jam-tart, and swallowed it, as though it had been a lump of
dripping.

Mrs. Curate was dreadfully irate. She didn't
faint, but she essayed to beat Boodlejack with
her parasol.

"The nasty ugly brute has eaten the dear
child's tart!" she cried, in doleful indignation.

When up spoke Crazy Jane, a young woman
who adores Boodlejack, and is not distinguished
for great reticence of tongue.

"He ain't nasty!" she cried. "He's washed
twice a week. He ain't ugly! He's a beauty,
he is. And as for eating the tart, there's two-
pence, and I wonder he didn't eat *you !*"

Of course we reproved Crazy Jane when this

conversation was reported to us. As for Boodle-jack, his misdeeds, it was admitted on all hands, merited sterner reprehension. The rosary pecca-dilloes were bad enough; but to be wanting in respect to an offshoot of the Church of England —that was unpardonable. Boodlejack was sen-tenced to be tied up; and a messenger was de-spatched to the village to buy him a chain and a kennel.

The gyves and a prison-house for him were pro-cured, and Boodlejack entered upon new condi-tions of existence. He howled at first, but speed-ily found consolation. He took to digging a grave with his paws by the side of his house, as though he had been a Trappist, and buried favor-ite bits of fat and bones of more than ordinary gristly succulence there.

He pined a little after the kitchen, whither he had been in the habit of repairing for the purpose of trying and smelling the joints as they went round on the spit, and unless restrained by Crazy Jane, of licking them. He found he could no longer bite people, but took it out in barking. He submitted to be called—in a slightly sarcastic tone—" poor old fellow," and " good doggy," by the postman, on whose calves, in bygone times, he had made many exemplary indentations. Per-haps the bitterest humiliation he had to endure was in the visits of Wee, the cat—a ginger-colored tom-tiger, addicted to fowling, ratting, field-mousing, and other out-door sports—who had formerly been a mere ball of fur for Boodlejack to toss about and trample on, but who would now come for an hour or two every day and sit in the sun over against Boodlejack's kennel, just out of the reach of his paws, eyeing him with sly and demure glances of malicious content-ment, as though to say, "Aha! you'll worry a poor ginger cat's life out, you will? How do you like a straw bed and a chain, eh?"

I don't think Boodlejack minded either much. He used to break his chain about three times a week, and essay to swallow some of the links. As for the kennel, although it was ten times his size, he very soon managed to drag it about after him. In the intervals, too, between the fracture of his fetters and their being mended, or new ones pro-cured, he was master of the situation; for he laughed at cord, and would have gnawed a cable through in half an hour.

At such times he would lead the domestic ani-mals a sad life, and again toss Wee up in the air, as the cow with the crumpled horn did the dog in the ballad; but it was very pleasant, never-theless, to see him gambolling on the lawn with a little boy who is now at school, knocking him down, and rolling him over, and barking furiously at the youngster, but in his wildest moments refraining from doing him the slightest hurt.

We have all grown older now, and sadder. I have given up the house, and live in a grim town brick-barn, where there are neither rats nor roses. And Boodlejack is pining in a back-yard, till I can find heart of grace to get out of this ab-horred London again, and let the big dog have his fling.

ON WHAT PEOPLE SHOULD HAVE FOR BREAKFAST.

AT last! After many months' beating about the bush, we come to the point; to a plain, practical, tangible issue. The last excuse for digression or desultory disquisition is taken away. If a man can't devote himself to the topic of breakfast while he is Breakfasting in Bed, of what use is it his breakfasting, or being in bed at all? What, indeed! save, perhaps, that he should go to sleep; which may be, after all, a more sensible manner of employing his time in a natural place of rest, than that of grumbling at a matutinal meal he should properly have partaken of in the parlor, or philosophising between the sheets when he should have been penning moral essays at his desk.

"On what people should have for breakfast?" Why didn't I grapple with that most important and little understood question last September? By this time I might have helped to clear away some mists of prejudice, to fish up some treacherously submerged torpedo of sophistry, to dredge away some bar of ignorance, to clear some chan-

nel leading into the harbor of truth, to mitigate
a nuisance, and to inaugurate a reform.   Or, very
probably, I might have done nothing whatever
of the kind ; and instead of rendering a service
to the cause of comfort and common sense, merely
stirred up a malignant controversy and provoked
a fruitless discussion.   To err is human ; with the
best intentions we ofttimes come to grief.

Look at the Right Honorable William Ewart
Gladstone and his proposition for licensing club-
houses as though they were gin-shops.   The right
honorable gentleman persuaded himself, no doubt,
that he was doing an uncommonly clever stroke
of business, and giving to his financial scheme of
'63 a brilliant gloss as a " poor man's budget."
" I'll take the Clubs," he said to himself (of course
in Attic Greek).   "The reproach of there being
one law for the rich and another for the poor,
shall be heard no longer.   What is sauce for the
goose shall be sauce for the gander.   The equi-
poise of justice shall be established between St.
James's and St. Giles's."   So he claps seventeen
pounds ten and five per cent. for liquor, and three
pounds ten and five per ditto for tobacco license
in to Pall Mall, and rubs his hands at the thought
of Whitechapel and Bethnal Green falling into
ecstasies at his impartiality ; and, behold, the
right honorable gentleman pleases nobody !

" It is a disgraceful imposition," yells St.

James's, in a rage; "it is a petty piece of tyranny, and Gladstone ought to be ashamed of himself. We don't sell wines, liquors, beer, or tobacco. We buy our own port, and our own cognac, and our own cigars out of our own funds, and don't want a licence to divide that which is our own among ourselves."

"It's all a something sham," mutters St. Giles's, surlily. "It's so much dust thrown in a cove's eyes. Mr. Gladstone he don't mean for to let the Peelers rummage about the Clubs; he ain't going to shut 'em during the hours of dervine service. He don't mean for to put an end to card-playing (and for precious high stakes, too) or to Darby sweeps among the nobs: and there's to be one law for the Clubs, and another for the 'Pig and Tinder-Box.'" Combined chorus of "He's a 'umbug and a do," from Whitechapel; and, "He has violated every pledge he ever gave to his order," from Pall Mall.

St. James's cuts Mr. Gladstone when he ventures to show himself at the Carlton, and sends him to Coventry if he puts in an appearance at the U. U.; and St. Giles's sneers at him as "a 'igh feller as gammons coves that he likes to do what's low."

Such is not unfrequently the fate of very clever and brilliant statesmen, who forget that

fluent rhetoric and specious casuistry are often
swamped for the want of a little candor and a
little sincerity.

I am writing at the risk of pleasing nobody;
but I passionately entreat you to believe that I
am both candid and sincere, and that on the
topic of Breakfast in Bed, at least you shall hear
nothing from me but words of honesty.

I went the other day to an eminent medical
man, and he, being sensibly of opinion that the
question of diet was of more importance than
that of pills or potions, asked me what I was in
the habit of taking for breakfast.

I answered : " At present, and as a rule, nothing but a cup of tea and the newspapers ; and
equally, as a rule, I can't get through either of
them. But in bygone days I used to make a very
excellent breakfast."

" What on ?" my medico searchingly inquired.

" Well," I returned, " I used to eat a mutton-
chop, or a rump-steak, or a good plateful from a
cold joint, or a couple of eggs broiled on bacon,
or a haddock, or a mackerel, or some pickled
salmon, or some cold veal-and-ham pie, or half a
wild duck, or a devilled partridge, with plenty
of bread-and-butter, or toast, or muffins, and perhaps some anchovy sauce, or potted char, or
preserved beef; the whole washed down by a
couple of cups of tea or coffee "——

He stopped me with a gesture of amazement, and a look of horror : " I wonder you didn't say a dish of chocolate and a glass of curaçoa, by way of a wind up," he exclaimed.

" No," I replied with modest ingenuousness ; I used to wind up with a pipe of bird's-eye. I didn't Breakfast in Bed in those days, and my digestion was pretty good, I thank you."

" And after these astounding confessions, you come to me," went on my doctor, " and grumble about your liver ! I am astonished that you have any left. You have been living in a manner that would kill half a dozen bricklayers' laborers. But there is time to reform. It is not yet too late. You should take for breakfast a very small quantity of dry toast, uniformly browned, and preferably without butter ; or if you do hanker after adipose matter, the very thinnest possible veneer of butter upon it. Then, if you have appetite enough for it, I would advise you to take a small quantity of bacon cut from the back, not the streaky bacon, and toasted before the fire, until all the oil has been expelled from the tissue. After that—you say you can't drink tea ?"

I stated that I could drink it by pailfuls, and was madly fond of it, but that it made me distressingly nervous.

" Coffee," he pursued, " is heating, unless you

have a minimum of the very finest Oriental berry, scientifically roasted and ground, to a maximum of the purest milk; and such things are difficult to obtain in London, or even in England. Can you drink homœopathic cocoa?"

I answered in a spirit similar to that which is said to have prompted the response of the young Irish gentleman when he was asked if he could play the fiddle; I said that I had no doubt of being able to drink homœopathic cocoa, if I tried.

"Then, try it," said my medico, "and come to me in three weeks' time."

I do not lose a moment in admitting that my adviser's breakfast *menu* was an admirably sensible one; but I very much doubt whether I should not have gone raving mad if I had adhered without variation to a repast consisting of toasted bacon, dry toast, and homœopathic cocoa. I tried it for a time, then gave it up. Bacon is a very nice thing. It is cruel and unjust, by incessantly consuming it, to have at last to loathe and abhor it. I tried my hardest to think it wholesome and appetizing; but to no purpose. I found myself rapidly approaching the detestation stage, and I don't mean to have any more bacon for breakfast for three months.

I have scarcely any need to point out that

variety in what you have for breakfast is the prime essential to enable you to eat any breakfast at all. Man was not meant to live on bread—nay, nor on toasted bacon, nor homœopathic cocoa—alone. If you don't vary his diet, if you don't give him something by way of a change, he will pine away, or refuse his victuals, and grow morose and refractory as a wild animal.

We have heard a great outcry within these latter days against the assumed luxurious manner in which criminals are fed in gaol. The rogues, it appears, live on savory soup, thickened with meal, and seasoned with vegetables, salt, and pepper. They have porridge and gruel, with milk and rich molasses, potatoes, boiled beef (free from bones) on stated days, and on others (the pampered Sybarites!) they are actually regaled with hot suet-pudding.

Has it any plums in it, I wonder? Only fancy giving "plum-duff" to garotters, and burglars, and pickpockets, and the atrocious scoundrels who have been convicted, under the new Poaching Act, of being found in possession of a rabbit's skin, or a pheasant's net. Now persons of practical experience, whether they be professed physiologists or not, are perfectly aware of these facts: that if you deprive a man of his liberty, and make him work at tasks uncongenial to his tastes, and subject him to a grinding and inquisitorial discipline, and feed him besides on bread and water, you will very soon drive him to idiocy, to murdering his gaoler, or to dashing his brains out against the walls of his cell.

A very short term of such a punishment is one of the most terrible to conceive in the whole arsenal of penal inflictions. In some cases it may be salutary; but, imposed for any lengthened period, it amounts simply to constructive murder. A criminal would infinitely prefer a thousand lashes to three weeks at Holloway or Wandsworth on "low diet."

Silly and irrational people, who can't see farther than the tips of their noses, think that because hard labor and the starvation system are efficacious when tried for a few days, criminals should be subjected to such a doom for months, for years, or for life. No prisoners could live, and no prison-authorities could enforce such a system in perpetuity.

Gaolers may look stern enough, but they are not vindictive or hard-hearted enough to meet all the requirements of the new school of philanthropy. The neo-philanthropists are indignant because the food is of good quality and is well cooked. Do they expect the county magistrates to insert advertisements in the papers, running, "Wanted, a dishonest contractor;" "Wanted, a scoundrelly carcass-butcher, who will supply so many hundred-weight of offal, various bones, and meat generally unfit for human food;" "Wanted, an idiot who can't cook;" "Wanted, a jackass who can turn a well-built prison-kitchen topsy-turvy?" Wherever you find order, cleanliness, a full supply of proper utensils, efficiency in the persons employed, and reasonably good qualities in the provisions supplied, there, I take it, must there be rations of well-cooked food, which those who know nothing about the matter term "luxurious." "Oh," cry the neo-philanthropists, "but we don't want any cooking at all for burglars and garotters. Feed the wretches once a day upon bread-and-water; and if they grumble, flog them well." I humbly submit that, since the world began, a diet exclusively composed of bread-and-water for persons in captivity has never been adopted, *as a permanency*, save where it was the deliberately-designed or avowed object to kill the captive. On the continent of Europe, in the most barbarously-managed convict-prisons, the galley-slaves are allowed to purchase articles of food, in addition to the rations allowed them by the State. The *forçats* of Toulon are fed on soup and beans and wine— all execrable in quality, no doubt, but still preserving them from despair by offering them some variety to an eternal regimen of ammunition-bread and muddy water. In the prisons of England, before John Howard's time, those incarcerated who had money were suffered to buy their own provisions, liquors, and tobacco, and really lived in a state somewhat resembling luxury, though of a coarse, riotous, and bestial kind. Those who had no money, literally rotted and died of inanition. Suppose the bread-and-water—and nothing but bread-and-water—system established permanently in a modern gaol. Do you know what the result would be after a few weeks' trial of the precious bill-of-fare? The prisoners would become living skeletons; on their knees and under their arms would rise dreadful glandular swellings. Their blood would turn to water, and that to an inconceivably horrible putrefaction. Try it, my lords and gentlemen. Try it, my neo-philanthropists. But, first of all, try the bread-and-water diet on yourselves, and tell me how you like it.

There is a prison at Munich where they give the best-behaved convicts, from time to time, a pint of beer. That mawkish draught of *Baerisch-Bier*, attainable, perhaps, once a month, is found to be the very highest and most efficacious incentive to exemplary conduct. At Gibraltar and Bermuda they used to give the felons a stick of Cavendish tobacco every week, and allow them a certain number of minutes every evening before

9

gun-fire to "blow their baccy." I have not the slightest doubt that this evening pipe has prevented many a mutiny and stifled many a murder in embryo. Practice has never been, and never will be on this side eternity, so remorseless and so vindictive as theory.

Thus the gentlemen who govern the victualling-department in prisons being, in nine cases out of ten, sensible, humane, and experienced men, who know what prisoners want and what they do not want much better than outside theorists, vary the breakfasts, dinners, and suppers of the unhappy persons confided to their charge to as great an extent as the exceedingly restricted dietary table will allow them to do. It is very easy to prate about convicts being pampered and coddled. It is also occasionally convenient to sneer at Sir Joshua Jebb and the Home Secretary, and drive them out into a wilderness of vituperation and misrepresentation, as scapegoats for our own shortcomings and blundering in time gone by; but I fancy that a couple of months' experience in the cell of a convict-prison would convince not a few of the virtuously-indignant-against-prisoners'-indulgence class, that the so-called pampering and coddling and luxury amount in the aggregate to a bare sufficiency of very plain, coarse, and distasteful food.

No beer, no gin, no fried fish, no baked Yorkshire-pudding, no hot eel-soup, no baked potatoes, no tripe, no cow-heel, no liver and bacon, no singed sheep's-head: a pitiless divorce from all these things, which, to the criminal tribes, are held eminently toothsome and savory. These deprivations are, to the felonious mind, ill compensated for by allotted rations of the simplest character, and from which spicy seasonings, and especially gravy—that rich juice so dear to all humanity—are inexorably banished. Cocoa-nibs may be all very nutritious and wholesome; but, ah! what are they to rum and milk? Molasses may be a comfort; but what is treacle in comparison with the dainties dispensed by the street-pieman?

We find among free men—among those classes whose members are not periodically locked up by the country for the country's good—that the want of variety in meals, but especially as regards breakfast, is surely productive of numerous evils to the body politic. Take schools, for instance. From year's end to year's end the hapless infants in academies for young gentlemen, or seminaries for young ladies, are condemned to a changeless round of thick bread-and-butter and sky-blue milk-and-water.

In a very few educational establishments, I am told—not one in half a hundred probably—the weakest of weak tea is served out; a mournful

decoction, in which luke-warm water preponder-
ates, in which the taste of brown sugar is faintly
felt, but in which the infusion of tea-leaves is in-
finitesimal.   Some sprays and buds of a strangely
herbaceous character float mournfully on the
surface of this so-called tea ; and the entire bev-
erage has a depressing and enfeebling effect on
the consumer.   Nevertheless such tea—albeit it
is but a scornful misnomer so to qualify it—is
reckoned a high and haughty luxury, to be re-
joiced in only in establishments of the highest
class ; and you may be tolerably certain that
the generous preceptors who give tea to their
scholars do not forget to put on something
extra for the use of the teapot in their half-yearly
bills.

But that bread-and-butter knows no change.
It may be that it is part of the private educational code to compel the housekeeper to cut the
young people's *tartines* of an unwieldy and almost unmasticatory density.   I suppose that it is
good for their little healths that the bread should
be stale.   "You are not quite so insane as to eat
new bread ?" my medical adviser said to me ; but
I forgot to introduce the query in its proper place.
I might have told him, but I didn't, that I always
ate new bread, and suffered accordingly.

There would be an end, of course, of all school-
discipline if any but the parlor-boarders and the

teachers were permitted to eat thin bread-and-butter, and a mutiny would be the infallible result of muffins. Of course the gradations of authority must be marked—in no place with more definite force than in a school.

When a child is decently behaved, he gets thick bread with very little butter on it. When he is naughty, he has dry bread, or, under certain circumstances of disgrace, no bread at all; but, at the other end of the scale, his pastors and masters, his good and wise schoolmaster or schoolmistress, revel in buttered toast; delicious cubes of spongy matter; *Rakat lakoum*, "lumps of delight," through every pore of which the oleaginous glue oozes. 'Tis a food for angels.

When I was at school in England, for a very short time, I am happy to say, the principal, with a touching humility, used to take his meals with us. He and his wife and daughter sat at a cross table: we had the immutable bread-and-butter and sky-blue; they had bacon, coffee, muffins, buttered toast. How often has my young soul yearned to make an onslaught on that well-filled upper end of the board—"groaning beneath all the delicacies of the season," as the reporters are accustomed to say of the annual dinner of the Sparkenhoe Farmers' Club—and carry off the middlemost layer of that mount of buttered toast, even at the risk of being hanged, expelled, or thrashed within an inch of my life for the rash and desperate deed!

I knew a schoolmaster once who, at the end of each half, and on the morning of the day they went home for the holidays, used to give his boys an egg for breakfast. Was it in pure liberality of soul that the donative was bestowed? or was it, the rather, the offspring of an artful *ruse* on the part of the astute pedagogue? Did he think to mollify obdurate boys, to condone bygone grievances, to put a plaster on wheals that were yet green (or black-and-blue) on boyish limbs, or to stifle nascent complaints which, to anxious and inquiring parents, he apprehended might be made? . I never knew; but it is certain that he gave his boys eggs with their thick bread-and-butter and their sky-blue, twice a year. The stratagem—if it was a stratagem—the generosity —if generosity indeed it was—were both thrown away.

Schoolboys are lamentably ungrateful. My friend's boys laughed his eggs to scorn. They imputed to him the worst and most interested motives. They declared the eggs to be musty. They forebore to eat, but pocketed them, and pelted one another with them in the playground. I remember a boy being caned, five minutes before he went home to his fond parents, for secreting an egg, on which happening inadvertently to sit, he squashed it, to the subversion of the good order of the establishment and the material injury of his pantaloons. The egg-trick ended in inglorious failure.

I think that if you were to canvass a large number of intelligent boys, you would find the majority against bread-and-butter a very numerous and decided one. For cake—plum or seedy—they have an ungovernable affection; bread and cheese even they will not spurn at; of puddings and pies they will devour, unless judiciously checked, incalculable quantities; but to bread-and-butter, unless driven by the pangs of absolute hunger, they are generally inclined to give a contemptuous go-by.

I was formerly aware of a boarding-school, where the morning and evening allowance to each boy was one entire slice cut right round a quartern loaf, and divided into four cubes or chunks. Now there was a rule in the school, that anybody having eaten his allowance, and craving more, should, on rising, clearing his voice, and asking deferentially, and in the German language, if he might have another piece of bread-and-butter, be entitled to an additional chunk. I think the formula ran thus: "*Herr Schlaghintern*"—this wasn't the schoolmaster's name; but 'twill serve—"*wollen Sie so gut seyn mir noch ein Stuck Butterbrod zu geben ?*" The condition was not a

very onerous one, and all the boys in the school
learnt German ; yet in the course of three halves,
I only knew the extra chunk to be claimed by
four boys.

¶ Big Jack Lazenby, whose father was a Baronet, and who was a fool—bless his honest, soft-
hearted memory !—spoke up for it, because another boy had made him a bet that he couldn't
utter four words in German without making
three blunders. He made two ; but these lapses
were sufficient to deprive him of the coveted
chunk. Little Harry Skipwith won it easily ;
but he gave it away to his next neighbor (Harry
was the boy who had a rich cake once a fortnight, and always brought five guineas to school,
at the commencement of a new half, as pocket-
money). Simon Dollamore, the rich City man's
son (he is now a richer man than his father), was
the densest of dunces at German ; but by labori-
ous plodding he contrived to master the mystic
sentence, and having obtained the chunk over
and above, sold it for a halfpenny. The com-
mercial operation was brought to light, and
Simon Dollamore, besides suffering corporal anguish on the palms of his hands from a ruler, was
informed no further proficiency he might attain
in the Teutonic tongue would avail in his obtaining extra bread-and-butter. The fourth claimant
was that luckless Gumbyle, whose father was

always bankrupt, and consequently neglected to
pay for the board and education of his son.
Gumbyle was egged-on one afternoon to rise and
claim the bread-and-butter bonus; but he hadn't
got further than " *wollen Sie so gut seyn,*" when
our revered preceptor marched up to him, boxed his ears, wondered at his impudence, and
sternly bade him sit down again and hold his
tongue.

If you come to the opposite sex, you will find
quite another feeling with regard to bread-and-
butter. I don't believe that any of the stories
told about the ravenous fondness of school-girls
for *Butterbrods* are exaggerated. I know a lady
who went to school at Kensington, and there the
servants put the bread-and-butter—when they
had cut it—for tea into a large clothes-basket to
be handed round, and even then the clothes-
basket would be found all too small. I hope I
shall not be contradicted by physiologists when
I assert, that in the majority of instances girls
have a far more voracious appetite than boys.
From nine to thirteen a girl would much sooner
have a slice of bread-and-butter than a hoop, a
doll, or a skipping-rope. This is why discreet
governesses are able entirely to dispense with
corporal punishment in girls' schools. A boy
doesn't care much about being deprived of a
meal; a girl does. If you were to ask her who-

9*

ther she preferred having her ears boxed or her knuckles rapped to going without her tea, she would answer—supposing her reply to be perfectly candid—in the affirmative. Starvation is a quiet, genteel, unobtrusive punishment. It causes no frenzied struggles, no violent howling. It is very cheap; and the establishment saves money by the culprits who are put *au pain sec.*

There comes a time, however, when we are our own masters and mistresses, and when it becomes our, often grievous, duty to order our own breakfasts. The question, "What shall we have for breakfast?" is a far more difficult one to solve than "What shall we have for dinner?" We can appeal to the cook, to Soyer, or Francatelli, or Dr. Kitchener, or Lady Clutterbuck, or to the wife of our bosom. We can remember some of the dainties of which we have partaken at friends' houses, or at places of public resort during the past week; or, at all events, we can throw ourselves on chops and steaks, or announce our intention of dining out. But breakfast brings a far different series of influences into play. The question is a momentous one, and you are easily stranded. If you are a family man, I will not assume that you can be, save in cases of extreme rarity, such a despicable and heartless ruffian as to breakfast away from home.

I know there are some men, lost to all sense

of domestic propriety—monsters in human form
—who, with a stony cynicism and unblushing
hardihood, will abandon their Lares and Penates
even while—the wretches !—the kettle is sputter-
ing on the hob and the urn simmering on the table.   These bold bad men will go shamelessly
down to their club and breakfast.   Their insolent
plea is, that an obsequious waiter will at once
pour into their ears a copious catalogue of appetising things that can be had for breakfast—boiled, grilled, stewed, devilled, and cold ; that everything is of first-rate quality, and served with
exquisite neatness and admirable expedition; that
all the newspapers, ready cut, are at hand; that
no single knocks from duns are possible; and that
a much better breakfast than can be had at home
costs much less money than it would among the
Lares and Penates.

Should you meet, my son, with any such
hardened men, follow my counsel, and avoid
them.   Their ways lead as surely to perdition as
a latch-key and a cigar-case lead to the unfa-
thomable abyss of Sir Cresswell Cresswell's court
and woe unutterable.

ON HAVING SEEN A GHOST AT HOX-
TON, AND THE VERY DEUCE
HIMSELF IN PARIS.

MISERY, we all know, makes a man acquainted with strange bedfellows; but the converse, which might be suggested to such a proverb, does not hold. Strange beds do not always make men miserable. The rather, sometimes, are they productive of ease and gratulation to the unaccustomed sleeper. It is in the nature of mutable and capricious man to grow weary of everything when its occupation is prolonged. Satisfaction begets sameness, and sameness satiety; and then we yawn and toss and tumble restlessly, and at last come to curse our day, as Job did.

Couch us on rose-leaves, and we begin to grumble for St. Lawrence's gridiron. Softly smother us in eider-down, and, with ungrateful shrug, we declare that we should like a heap of red-hot coals by way of a change. When St. Louis was dying, he caused himself to be stretched on a bed of ashes. Was that act of mortification due to pure, virtuous asceticism, think you, or to sheer weariness of soft feather-beds and silken hangings? There are seasons when the roomiest four-poster, the snuggest Arabian, pall upon and disgust us; when we would gladly exchange the fluted silk of the alcove for the whitewashed walls of the hospital dormitory.

Mattresses, paillasses, and feather-beds, bolsters, pillows, and counterpanes, are all very well; but, ah, for the delights of a swinging hammock or a camp-bedstead!—ah, for the invigorating change of a night in the open air, with the stars for a canopy, and nothing but a buffalo-robe between yourself and mother earth!

How glorious it is, for example, to retire to rest with a carpet-bag under your head, and wake up in the morning your cranium a mass of abnormal bumps, embossed there by contact with subjacent hair-brushes, pomatum-pots, and boot-heels!

How charming to repose by the bivouac-fire, and discover on the morrow that your toes have been half burnt off! And the pleasant nights when you don't go to bed at all!—when you pace the deck, a cigar between your lips; or are jolted from side to side of a railway carriage; or sink into a troubled slumber in the *impériale* of a diligence, with your head on the shoulder of the *conducteur*, who very summarily shakes you off every time the coach stops to change horses.

During the whole of the month of June just past, I have been sleeping in very strange beds, and eating stranger breakfasts in them. I have been a wanderer on the face of the earth, and have mooned half over Europe. I have drunk the waters of unwonted rivers. The Seine I have seen, the Marne, the Meuse, the Scheldt, the Rhine, the Moselle, and the Necker; yea, and the Maine, the Inn, the Adige, the Arno, the Po, and the Rhone.

Several nights, a dozen, perhaps, I have passed in my clothes, and without thinking of sleep; but on all other occasions I have Breakfasted consistently in Bed. It is the fashion in outlandish countries so to do; at least to consume breakfast number one between the sheets. Breakfast number two, the *déjeûner à la fourchette*, I cautiously abjure, fearing apoplexy.

I came abroad, when May was on the wane, with two brisk and valiant young Englishmen, determined to do at Rome—whither we didn't go —as the Romans did, and at Paris as the Parisians. They astounded and humbled me, an old and experienced traveller as I deemed myself, by their fluent acquaintance with Continental customs, especially those relating to eating and drinking.

" *Café au lait* and bread-and-butter in bed at 8 A. M., of course," quoth Englishman number one. "And then," pursued the second Anglo-Saxon, in loud and strident tone, "at half-past twelve or so, we go out to a *café*, and have our regular breakfast—our *déjeûner à la fourchette :* eggs on the plate, a *biftek aux pommes*, and so forth, and a bottle of Bordeaux apiece."

In tremulous horror I shrunk from this alarming programme. Protest I dared not, for my Englishmen were stout and strong, and would have beaten me; but I meekly represented that I was accustomed to consume only two meals a day; that to partake of animal food at noon would be about equivalent to signing my death-warrant; that, in my opinion, after a substantial breakfast, a Christian man wanted nothing but a crust of bread and a glass of wine till dinner-time; and that to imbibe the contents of a bottle of Bordeaux for lunch would surely cause me to spin round like a tee-totum on the Boulevard, or commit an aggravated assault on the nearest *sergent de ville.*

"Milksop !" I heard one of my companions murmur. "Hypocrite !" muttered the other. "I told you so. Coats of the stomach quite gone. Healthy appetite lost for ever. Wants to slink out and breakfast by himself on raw artichokes and absinthe."

To clear myself from these cruel aspersions, I gave up my point, and fell into their ways, at the imminent risk of tumbling down with a *coup de sang*. Ye Lars and Lemures, how those two young men ato and drank! And yet they seemed none the worse for their excesses. I love them both, I esteem them both ; but I declare I felt a grim satisfaction when they departed from me, and left me to continue my journey alone and practise a sullen abstemiousness, for which I feel none the better.

So I took to Breakfasting in Bed at any hour I chose, and reading in bed, and day-dreaming in bed, and talking to myself in bed, and sometimes groaning in bed, and occasionally, as foreign fire-insurances were no concern of mine, smoking in bed. There is much virtue in an early morning cigarette. If you presumed to smoke in bed in England, those who became acquainted with your habit would declare you to be a Socinian, or a Freethinker, or hint that you poisoned your wife, or were on the brink of bankruptcy. But there are, happily, so many things you can do abroad which you cannot do at home. Such, at least, has been my experience. There are advantages *pro* and privations *contra*, I grant. On the one hand, you escape from tutelage, from being scolded, from being asked what you would like for dinner, from receiving penny-post letters and morning visits, from being told that the Gas has called again, and that the coals are out, and from reading the "Saturday Review" on your last literary performance.

On the other hand, there is no one to "share your cup," or cheer it, or pour it out, or sweeten it, or throw it at you. There is no one to part your hair or tie your scarf. There is no one to give the soft answer which turneth away wrath, or to utter the wrathful taunt which the soft answer assuages—sometimes.

On the whole, I think it a pleas mt thing, and useful and wholesome, to stay away now and then from your bed and board. 'T:s sweet to hear the dulcet tones of "Willie, we have missed you," on your return; and if your name doesn't happen to be Willie, and you don't hear the dulcet tones above mentioned, it is, at least, edifying to the philosophical mind to discover how comfortably the world has gone on in your absence, and how charmingly people have managed without you.

· This morning I am Breakfasting in Bed at an hotel on the Boulevard Poissonnière, Paris, and I cry "Ha! ha!" over my *café au lait;* for, with the consistency of inconsistency, I have by this time grown tired of wandering, and strange breakfasts, and strange beds, and am longing for the old London treadmill, and the old delightful condition of always wanting to do what I like and never being allowed to do it. I cry "Ha!

ha !" for this night I am bound to London town,
no more to leave it till I cross the Atlantic wave,
the which, for aught I know, may transform
itself betwixt this and August into the dull
rolling billow of the leaden-hued Styx. I
besought my bed-maker, who is of the male persuasion—and, like the majority of his brother
chambermen, a strong politician, a very civil
and obliging fellow, and a shameless rogue—I
besought Antoine to fetch me "Figaro."

This is Thursday morning, and a new number
is due. Antoine is *Luca fa presto* in his movements—when he's paid to be quick—and with
celerity he brings me "Figaro"—not the witty
barber of Seville, but the scarcely less witty
journal non politique of Paris. It is delightful
reading in bed. I am skimming over the *chron-
ique* and the *nouvelles à la main* when my eye
lights on the following paragraph :

"M. Lambert Thiboust, dramatic author, and
M. Hostein, ditector of the Théâtre du Châtelet,
have left Paris for London, in order to investi-
gate a trick (*un truc*) which is said to have had
great success on the English stage. We will say
nothing of the nature of this trick in order to
detract from the astonishment which will surely
be created by its appearance in Paris. Nor as
yet will we mention the piece in which the said
trick is to be introduced. It is one of Miss

Aurora's Secrets." (*C'est le secret de Miss Aurore.*)

What is this wonderful trick? I asked myself. Has anybody succeeded in walking into a quart bottle, or making the Soho Theatre pay, since I ·left London? Have MM. Lambert Thiboust and Hostein gone to study the art of trickery under Mr. Diana Boucicault?

By the way, M. Hostein, your last visit to London was not of a very gratifying character. Do you remember the year? It was '48. Do you remember the piece you produced at Drury Lane Theatre? It was "Monte Christo." Do you remember the result? It was a riot.

A stormy period was '48. Kings were being toppled off their thrones all over Europe, and "Monte Christo" was hooted off the stage of old Drury in the midst of an uproar to which the O. P. row must have been angelic calmness.

Long I wondered and pondered over this mysterious *truc*. Had it anything to do with the "infamous truck system?" Could it claim kindred with Mr. Gladstone's budget, or Mr. Disraeli's policy? Was it the bottle-trick, or the skeleton-trick, or the globe-of-gold-fish trick of our conjurors and pantomimists? Surely, no. Those amusing deceptions are notoriously of foreign origin, and we have but taken French leave in adapting them on our boards. At last

I saw a clue, and cried out Eureka. The Secret
of Miss Aurore! Why, under that queer title
"Figaro" is now publishing, in a bi-weekly supplement, a translation of the famous novel of
"Aurora Floyd;" and who but the translator told
me that M. Hostein is about to produce the said
Secret de Mademoiselle Aurore as a grand
melodramic spectacle at the Châtelet, and has
positively engaged poor old Frederic Lemaître
to fill the part of "the Softy." The *true* must be
the admired Ghost-trick of Professor Pepper and
Mr. Dircks; and, with the characteristic hardihood and scornful independence of the unities
of proprietors and the probabilities of French
dramatic authors, M. Lambert Thiboust is about
to present the Parisian public with Aurora Floyd
and a Ghost into the bargain. Poor Miss Aurora!
poor Mrs. J. Mellish! Who would ever have
thought of that vivacious young lady addicting
herself to spirit-rapping?

Rendering due justice to the genius and enterprise of MM. Lambert Thiboust and Hostein,
and only marvelling as to the particular part of
Miss Braddon's romance into which they could
contrive to pop Professor Pepper's Ghost, my
vagrant thoughts revert to Hoxton town, in the
borough of Finsbury, England. 'Twas there,
last May, I saw the real, Pepperian, hair-stand-
on-end-compelling Ghost. But five weeks since!

It seems an age to me; and even, dramatically speaking, it seems a year.

Theatres and theatres have I beheld since Mr. Lane gave me a box for the Britannia. The Paris Grand Opera, the Cirque, and the Châtelet, I took first. Next came the clean, commodious theatre at Frankfort-on-the-Main, where I heard Meyerbeer's "Dinorah" and Gounod's "Faust." Then I dropped down to Munich, and saw "Guillaume Tell" from the stalls of the magnificent Maximilian Theatre. Then the Genius of Vagabondism wafted me through the Tyrol, and down to Verona, and landed me at Venice; where, alas! I found the sumptuous Fenice shut up these five years, the San Benedetto doomed also to chronic closing, and only one little trumpery dramatic temple open, the Teatro Malibran, admission to the boxes thirty kreutzers (about eightpence).

What do you think they were playing at the Teatro Malibran? *Il Segreto di Miladi Audlei*—"Lady Audley's Secret!" In the official Gazette of Venice—a stern journal, full of rugose decrees from Vienna, and alarming police-edicts—I found the *feuilleton* to be an Italian translation of an English novel. For completeness' sake, it should have been either "Aurora Floyd" or "Lady Audley's Secret;" but it happened, for a wonder, to be something else. It was only Mrs. Henry Wood's "East Lynne."

Back, back to Hoxton, fugitive remembrances.
Hoxton! where is Hoxton? I declare I don't
know. "Hear him!" Hircius and Spungius
yelp. "Hear the base upstart plead ignorance
as to the whereabouts of Hoxton. Hear him try
to ape the dead cynic who asked where Russell
Square was. Hoxton, and be hanged to him!
As though he never ate fried fish, or tramped
about, shoeless, there." Well, H. and S., I *don't*
know where Hoxton is. It is somewhere near
the City Road, I think; but I have not the least
idea in what particular locality.

I wrote to Mr. Lane, and with his customary
urbanity he wrote back to say that he should be
glad to see me at Hoxton. As I was pressed for
time, and there happened to be a lady in the case
on the appointed evening, I had a cab from
Bloomsbury to Hoxton, and I had a cab back;
and, from that day to this, I have not been able
to acquire more than the vaguest and mistiest
notion of what Hoxton is like, or where it is
situated, or what are the manners and customs of
its inhabitants.

I apprehend, however, that there must be
several millions of people in Hoxton. The child-
dren swarm there to such an extent, that had.
Professor Pepper and Mr. Dircks, C.E., raised
the ghost of the late Rev. Mr. Malthus in lieu of
that of the —— at the Britannia, the spectre of

the famous anti-population theorist would have turned green with rage at the sight of so many human beings promising adolescence. Anti-Malthusian doctrines were happily at a discount at Mr. Lane's establishment, whither the millions (more or less) of Hoxton had on the particular May night in question despatched a varied deputation, a few thousands strong, to see the Ghost. There were a great many children in the theatre; but they were all remarkably quiet, hushed to stillness probably by apprehension, by anticipation of the Phantom. If there were any babies in arms among the audience, their mothers and nurses must have taken very good care of them; for, from beginning to end of the entertainment, I heard not one squall. Perhaps these Hoxtonian infants, with a wisdom beyond their years, were aware of the salutary edicts levelled by the management against babyhood of a nature so vociferous as to interfere with the general comfort of the spectators. Perhaps they stuffed their little fists into their little mouths, held their little breaths, and cheerfully martyrized themselves, in order not to mar the decorous procession of the Ghost. At any rate, they were edifyingly undemonstrative; and if, when they returned home, they compensated for their prolonged taciturnity by roarings the most deafening and squallings the most ear-piercing, small blame to the babies of Hoxton, say I.

It would be unjust to deny the grown-up portion of a closely-packed auditory a well-merited good word. I am not of those who habitually and glibly compliment the working-classes on their "exemplary good behavior," and who think it rather a marvellous and phenomenal circumstance, when two or three thousand honest and hard-working people are gathered together, that they do not immediately proceed to poke their fingers through the pictures, mutilate the statues, smash the glass cases, root up and trample down the flower-beds, and tear up the benches of the galleries, museums, palaces, and theatres in which they are permitted gratuitously or by payment to disport themselves. I do not volunteer such conventional panegyrics, because I hold them to be perfectly uncalled for and grossly impertinent, and because I am bold enough to think that the working-classes know quite as well as the non-working-classes can do how to behave themselves in public and in private, and do, not unfrequently, behave themselves a great deal better.

Still was there something in the aspect of this vast Britannia throng calling for something more than trite and perfunctory commendation. It was a Saturday night, and the majority of the working people there must have had their wages in their pockets, or—the next thing to it—in the pockets of the buxom wives who, as a praiseworthy rule, accompanied them. I did not see, nor indeed could any one else, unless provided with the double-million magnifiers recommended by Mr. Samuel Weller, any disposition on the part of this dense throng in fustian and corduroy to rush out to the nearest beer-shops and gin-palaces to squander their ready money in intoxicating liquors, to return in a frantic state to batter and bruise their wives and families with pint pots, legs of tables, and other lethal weapons of a blunt nature; and then, after pawning their saws and chisels, and running up scores on account of next week's wages, to assure Mr. Solly, and the editor of the "British Workman," and other friends of the enslaved and oppressed, that "the drink had done it all," and that the only remedy for this alarming state of things was to petition the Legislature for the immediate enactment of the Maine liquor-law, and the wholesale closing of public-houses on week-days in general, and from Saturday night to Monday morning in particular. I opine that, among the working-classes—as among the middle classes, and the "upper middle classes" (wherever they may be), and the upper classes, including the most ineffably Brahminical, with the yellowest streaks of caste on their foreheads—there is, has been, and ever will be, a certain per centage of human hogs who choose to wallow in their own or the nearest licensed victualler's stye, and to go to the devil in their

10

own way. Of the Hoxton hogs, the average per centage were doubtless getting howling, snivelling, or dumb drunk at the adjacent public-houses. It is certain that they were not at the Britannia to see the Ghost; and it is equally certain that, under even the slightest influence of alcohol, they would not have been allowed to pass the outer barriers of the theatre.

The occupants of the "auditorium" were, as a rule, a great deal soberer than I have often seen, after dinner, the occupants of stalls and the back seats of the dress-circle at West-End theatres; but their sobriety was due to no teetotal code, to no compulsory Lane liquor-laws. There is an abundance of refreshment-counters attached to the Britannia Theatre. Beer between the acts is a recognised institution, and is extensively drunk on the premises. There is even a smoking-room, just as there is to be a *fumoir* at the new Paris Opera House; nor, I believe, are those whose purses will support the expense debarred from partaking of hot and cold brandy-and-water, or champagne, or Johannisberg, or Hippocras, or Imperial Tokay, if they like to order it, and to pay for it, and it happen to be in the stock of the Britannia cellars.

There was a great deal to be seen before the great attraction of the evening—the Ghost—was manifest. There was the house itself to gaze at, densely thronged, as I have said, but not uncomfortably so. In boxes as in gallery, in stalls as in pit, every one had ample scope and verge to sit at ease, and, in the intervals of the pieces, and at the close of the entire entertainment, to circulate and depart without let or hindrance. The " vomitoria," as Mr. Boucicault would call them, were numerous, and skilfully constructed; and it was quite wonderful to see, when the night's diversions had been brought to a close, in how short a period of time—a few moments only it seemed—the immense area, so lately black with humanity, was deserted. Then there were the decorations of the house to admire—decorations, fittings, and appointments all handsome, tasteful, and commodious, without being either prodigal or meretricious.

The stage of the Britannia is really superb both for size and proportions:—the width of the proscenium surprising. There is a very artistically-executed drop-curtain; and of the scenery, properties and dresses, all that I saw was not only creditable, but of a degree of excellence which would by no means have suffered by comparison with the haughtiest theatres of the West. And why should it so have suffered, I should like to know? The Britannia audience know a good thing when they see it, quite as well as other people; nay, can at times be curiously apprecia-

tive and nicely critical. "We doesn't expect
grammar at the Wic," once cried out a gentleman in the gallery, at the well-known home of
transpontine melodrama when an unusually ill-
set scene was put upon the stage—"we doesn't
expect grammar ; *but you might jine your flats.*"

The Britannia audience are in advance of the
Victorians, and would certainly resent, not only
badly-joined, but carelessly-painted " flats ;" nay,
more than this, from the slight experience I have
had of the establishment, I am inclined to think
that grammatical accuracy is by no means a drug
in the market at Hoxton, and that very unmis-
takable signs of disapprobation would be apparent were Priscian's head to be broken too frequently and in too outrageous a manner in the
course of one evening.

I frankly confess, that of the great spectacu-
lar, non-natural, preternatural, supernatural, and
thoroughly Hoxtonian melodrama of "The Widow
and the Orphan ; or, Faith, Hope and Charity"—
if, at this distance of time and place, I am able
to quote the title aright—I am unable to give
anything beyond a very confused and involved
account. To tell the truth, I couldn't make anything of the piece. It was too much for me.
The plot was too complicated, the action too
rapid, the incidents were too grandiose for my in-
tellectual capacity.

I am destitute of the faculty of comprehensive criticism. I cannot understand an aggregate. Give me a minute point, a subdivided section, and I can concentrate my attention on it and discourse about it, *tant bien que mal*. But the task of comprehending "The Widow and the Orphan" was ten times too Herculean for me. I know that the widow was a very neat and dapper widow —as widows go—brimming over with moral sentiments of the most unobjectionable character; in short, a pattern to all widows, past, present and to come. There were two orphans, also, I think. One was meek, mild, uncomplaining; the other sprightly, vivacious, and facetious, and "keeping her pecker up"—to employ an expression which would be intolerably vulgar, I am afraid, even at Hoxton (why even at Hoxton? is there no slang in high places?)—under the most adverse circumstances. I think the part of the sprightly and vivacious orphan was filled by Mrs. Lane, the manager's wife, and the lady to whom much of the admirable discipline, organization, and tasteful arrangement which have made the Britannia a model to all London theatres is due.

I am not certain, but this I opine, that the sprightly and vivacious orphan could be also, upon occasion, sentimental and pathetic, and was throughout graceful and ladylike. Then there was a baronet in Hessian boots, and a wig and a cocked-hat, if my remembrance serves me, and who was, perhaps, one of the wickedest, cruellest, and most hypocritical old miscreants ever permitted to infest the neighborhood of Hoxton, or anywhere else.

What showers of five-cent pieces and decayed apples they would have cast on his congener on the *Boulevard du Crime !* What a storm of peanuts would have assailed him at the Bowery? The less demonstrative Britannia audience were content to shudder at his enormities, without pelting him. To this most depraved and flagitious member of the aristocracy perjury was a pastime, and bearing false-witness a *bagatelle.* He lied himself black in the face habitually. His profligacy was equal to his perfidy. Who but he locked up one of the orphans on a perfectly unsustainable charge, thereby laying himself open to an action and heavy damages for false imprisonment, and then—the hardened old sinner!—wanted to "square" matters by marrying her? It is needless to say that his proffered hand was disdainfully refused by the wronged and outraged orphan.

It was this baronet who saw—but I am forestalling matters. This hoary-headed villain had a son—at least, he hadn't a son, for the young man turned out in the last act to be somebody else's—whom he was continually cursing, betraying, cheating, turning out of doors, and cutting off with a shilling; adding, besides, insult to injury, by calling him abusive names, and threatening him with his walking-stick. There were two more villains in the piece:—one a returned convict in high boots and a hairy cap, who looked Norfolk Island all over, with a dash of Bermuda, a tincture of Swan River, and a pervading flavor of the New Cut; the other a desperate ruffian in black whiskers, a red waistcoat, and leather gaiters, who, in the first instance, was ready for any crime, from pitch-and-toss up to manslaughter—nay, beyond that last-named offence, for he devoted himself to assassination as blithely as Saltabadil in "Le Roi s'Amuse," and *tuait à la campagne, ou en ville.*

Ultimately, be it recorded, to the honor of human nature and the confusion of the theorists who maintain that crime is incurable, this abandoned scoundrel became softly and sentimentally virtuous—quite a pastoral character, in fact— and was instrumental in rescuing one of the orphans who had been pitched down a well, recovering a stolen lease, and bringing the depraved baronet to justice.

Then there was a comic groom, who afterwards became an agriculturist, and who elicited shouts of laughter both in his livery cockade and top-

boots, and in his smock-frock and wide-awake.
I am glad to say that he made my sides ache,
too, in a most unaccustomed manner, although I
did not in the least know what I was laughing
at. There were two bailiffs, and, if I mistake
not, some of the county police concerned in the
later transactions of the evening.

There was a house on fire—a very carefully-
managed conflagration, in the midst of which Mr.
Hodges' fire-engine, or its twin brother, made its
appearance on the stage; and I fancied that I
could discern among the attendant supers the
agile form of the Duke of Sutherland. If his
Grace wasn't there, the Earl of Caithness must
have been. Finally, there was a mysterious individual of ripe—almost overripe—age, with very
thin legs, and a smock-frock very much patched,
a pillicock hat, and a basket containing either
rags, bones, or chickweed at his back.

This ancient party was continually stumping
about with a crooked staff, interfering with everybody's business, but with ultimately beneficent
intentions. He was a violent democrat, and
when the baronet called him an " old pauper,"
made that unfeeling and flagitious person the
butt of some very stinging sarcasms against the
vices and folly of the governing classes. In the
end, it turned out that he wasn't a pauper, but a
real gentleman of the highest respectability, only

he had "something on his mind," owing to his not having behaved well to his deceased wife, or his deceased wife not having behaved well to him : I couldn't exactly make out which, but either eventuality is feasible. All came right at last. The old gentleman flung by his basket of rags, bones, or chickweed, and appeared in irreproachable coat, flapped waistcoat, and smallclothes. The good people were all made happy, and the bad people transported. Vice was trampled beneath the iron heel of the high-low of Virtue ; and Faith, Hope, and Charity, came, like the Hebrew children, unharmed from the fiery furnace, and were triumphant.

To have witnessed such a spectacle could not perhaps have done anybody's æsthetic and elastic taste much good ; but I am an antediluvian sprat if it could have done anybody's morals any harm.

Stop, there was a kind of ante-climax, an intercalary tableaux, the apotheosis of somebody— the widow, I think—in which, after the famous model represented at the Princess's in " Faust and Marguerite," under Mr. Charles Kean's management, an emancipated spirit was seen ascending to realms of bliss, encircled by flying Cupids and flying *coryphées*, all brilliantly illumined by the electric light. This tableau, which, viewed spectacularly, was exceedingly effective, was

10*

greeted, I need not say, with the most vehement
applause from the audience.

But the Ghost; the Ghost was the thing destined to make us all open our eyes in blank
amazement, and to sear, as with a red-hot
iron, the conscience of the guilty baronet. He
had retired to his study with two pair of wax-
candles, an oaken escritoire, and a couple of
tables and high-backed chairs, to meditate and
mature fresh deeds of villany. Conscience smote
him ; but he defied her. Then Conscience came
up again in the guise of a Ghost, and again and
again, Ghost after Ghost ; and the baronet yelped
with terror. Conscience had him on the hip.
Conscience made his spinal marrow assume the
consistency of vanilla ice. Conscience brought
out the cold drops on his hitherto brazen and
unblushing brow.

I am not bound to register what my conscience
said, or to speculate upon what other people's
consciences said to them, on the occasion ; but I
avow that, although I knew the whole thing to
be a clever optical delusion, devised, or patented,
or registered by Mr. Dircks, C.E., and Professor
Pepper, I shook all over, and my feet felt gelid in
my anklejacks. There was Death with his dart—
Death in the guise of a grisly skeleton. I didn't
mind him much, for his anatomical development
did not appear to me to be quite accurate, and

he looked a little too much like a King of Terrors on pasteboard. Still the suddenness of his appearance, and the more wonderful instantaneousness of his disparition, made my heart tumble abnormally on its axis.

But when the Ghost of the widow came up, lurid and menacing, seemingly palpable and tangible, yet wholly unsubstantial—when she pointed to the baronet and reproached him with his sins, and cried, "Ha! ha!"—and when, like a flash of summer lightning, she disappeared—I too, knowing always this to be a clever optical delusion, shook more than ever in my shoes, and felt unwonted moisture on my forehead.

This was the Ghost I saw at Hoxton. This is the Ghost, I presume, that all London has gone wild about since its first appearance at the Polytechnic—the Ghost that is now walking at the Adelphi, and that is speedily to harrow up the souls of the Parisians.

As I finish my Breakfast in Bed this morning, the Hoxton Ghost rises up before me, vivid and sparkling as ever, and I laugh at the clumsy trickery of · the *Pilules du Diable* I saw last night at the Porte St. Martin. "The Devil is an ass," quoth rare Ben Jonson; and surely the P. S. M. *diablerie* was of the most asinine description. The Ghost, after all, is the thing. *Vive le revenant!* But there is one thing which contin-

ues to puzzle me desperately. How on earth, or
under the earth, or over the earth, will MM.
Lambert Thiboust and Hostein contrive, with
anything like that common reason which is said
to be existent even in the roasting of eggs, to introduce the Polytechnico-Britannia Ghost into
Le Secret de Miss Aurore?

ON THE DISCOVERY IN ONE'S WAIST-COAT-POCKET OF SOME BONES OF UNUSUAL CHARACTER.

BONES, forsooth, and in one's waistcoat-pocket too! What next? the outraged reader will probably desire to know. But this is a plain, unvarnished statement; and the fact is as I set it down. *Bones of an unusual character were discovered, while I was Breakfasting in Bed on the 2d of July, 1863, in a certain waistcoat-pocket, and the waistcoat to which that pocket belonged was mine.*

Granted that such an article of male habiliment is not precisely the place where, under ordinary circumstances, you would look for osseous fragments. The study of comparative anatomy seldom leads a man so far as to induce him to convert his pockets into depositories for bones. Besides, I am neither Professor Owen nor a medical student. You can keep a skeleton in your closet; many persons nurture a serpent in their bosoms; and more than one member of my acquaintance habitually wears a bee in his bonnet;

but, for all this, it certainly seems wanting in
congruity to turn your vest into a Golgotha.
Whence and why these organic remains in the
locality above mentioned?

It is nevertheless undeniable that men do carry
very strange and surprising things about with
them. "The Mysteries of Men's Pockets" would
furnish materials for a book fraught with direful
interest. There are secrets hidden in the calico-
lined recesses of broadcloth and shrunken tweed
that would make you shudder if revealed. Yonder rosy-cheeked man, with the simple-minded
and unsophisticated countenance, who seems so
pleasurably intent on a portrait of the Princess
Alexandra in a newsvender's window—what do
you think his pockets contain? Nothing less
than two pairs of handcuffs, a revolver, a truncheon with a brass crown at the top, and a warrant to take you up, my felonious friend. He is
Inspector Weasel of the Detective Force; and,
absorbed by the royal portrait as he appears to
be, his actual eyes are fixed on William Sykes,
Esquire, late of Bermuda, then of Portland, and
now of Whitechapel, out of any trade or occupation save burglary, who is lurking over the way,
and upon whom he will, within the twinkling of
a truncheon, incontinently pounce. And W. S.,
Esq., himself? Who but the Inspector, to see
William arrayed as a peaceable journeyman-car-

penter, or innocuous bricklayer's laborer, or inoffensive railway-porter, would imagine that,
lying perdu in William's pocket of velveteen or
fustian, there were such unconsidered trifles as a
jemmy or two and a couple of centrebits, a bunch
of skeleton-keys, a crape-mask, a knuckle-duster,
and three inches and a half of wax-candle—the
entire apparatus of William's little housebreak-
ing business, in fact?

Behold that down-looking individual, who in
apparel reminds you equally of a charity schoolmaster and a retired tradesman in a Dissenting
neighborhood. · Ask him what he has got in his
pocket.   A tract? a hymn-book? Not a bit of it.
A coil of new rope; and you will swing in it,
by bloodthirsty friend, as sure as the down-
looking gentleman's name is Calcraft, next Monday morning.   If we changed the venue from
pockets to parcels, revelations as astounding
could be made.

Is it possible ever to forget that horribly facetious story of Mr. Greenacre, lightly tripping out
of the omnibus with a bundle of something in a
blue bag under his arm, and remarking, with an
air of banter to the conductor as he handed him
his fare, that he really thought he ought to have
paid for two? The simple cad did not comprehend
his meaning then; but the gist of Mr. Greenacre's
joke was apparent when it afterwards came out

that the blue bag contained the head of Hannah
Brown.

It was on a smooth highway once, in mid-
spring and in the pleasantest part of the pleasant
county of Kent, that, with Eugenius and Orlando,
I careered in an open fly. The sun shone; the
birds sang; the corn waved. We had lunched
well, and proposed to dine even better. We
laughed, and chanted carols of revelry. All at
once came a rattling along the road, and a chaise-
cart, drawn by a plump horse, passed us. There
were two policemen in the cart, two merry mu-
nicipals, who now giggled, and now guffawed, as
they retailed, perchance, the scandal of the station, or girded at the inspector. One smoked a
short pipe; the other, who held the reins, chew-
ed the cud of sweet fancies in the shape of a
flower. Why should not policemen enjoy themselves as well as other people? There jogged
between them, in the cart, a certain jar of stone-
ware, with a piece of leather tied over the top;
and, striking up an impromptu acquaintance with
the official men, as by the freemasonry of the
road we were warranted in doing, we joked them
on what the jar might contain, playfully suggesting pickles, beer, or Old Tom, and challenging
them to open and allow us to partake of its contents. "I don't think you'd like it, master," the
policeman who wasn't driving, remarked, re-

moving the short pipe from his lips. "What's in that jar ain't nice, I fancy. *It's just the stomach of the old gentleman as was pisoned at Maidstone, and we're takin' it to be hanalyzed.*" That day we laughed no more.

The mention of this alarming occurrence does not, perhaps, tend to the elucidation of the question of domestic paleontology which forms the subject-matter of this Paper. You have my admission that bones—strange bones—were found in my waistcoat-pocket (a dress-waistcoat, too, *moire antique*); but how came those bones, or any bones at all, there, where no bones should be? In this wise, candor compels me to relate. I presume that a family-man—a person, in short, who is habitually under the disciplinary control and supervision of other persons who torment him for his good, and make his life miserable in order that he may be happier afterwards—need experience no feeling of humiliation in the knowledge that the wearing-apparel he has cast off is, as a rule, searched before he breakfasts the next morning. If he *do* feel humiliated, it doesn't much matter. He will be searched all the same. You think, when you have laid your watch, purse, pocket-book, pencil-case, latch-key, and so forth on your dressing-table at night, that you have made a clean sweep of your pockets. " Get all that nonsense out of your head," as

C. J. Fox said to Napoleon. The domestic
inquisition will be at work ; the domestic search-
warrant will be issued ; you are sure to have forgotten something in your pockets, and that something is sure to be discovered before you rise
again. A due consciousness of this inevitability
has led some astute sages to select secret hiding-
places in their garments calculated to elude the
strictest search. To have secret drawers made in
the heels of your boots, and in the event of their
being discovered, to declare they are spur-boxes,
may be, perhaps, going a little too far ; and
occult pockets in the lining of the back of your
coat, are apt, if you use them as receptacles for
personal effects, to give you the appearance of
being humpbacked; but the inside of an umbrella
is not a bad place for the concealment of trifles
you don't wish discovered—say, the smoking-cap
you purchased at Mrs. Pelham Villars' stall at
the fancy fair in aid of the funds for the Repent-
ant Ragamuffins' Turkish Baths Association. Let
your umbrella be an ugly one, so that the searching officers of your household may not feel
inclined to borrow it.

An umbrella, however, is easily lost ; and the
lining of your hat may be, after all, the very best
hiding-place for things you are desirous of keeping perdu, such as your proofs of Rafaelle's
Madonnas, your certificate as a member of the

Anti-Tobacco Association, your temperance medal, and the private addresses of the widows and orphans in New Zealand and the Valleys of Uganda, to whom you have (in the charity and philanthrophy of your heart) allocated small annual pensions. Why not lock these articles up? you may ask. Bah! puerility! overween-ing fatuity! As if other people were not always in the possession of means for opening your drawers and strong-boxes?

Women have all acquired, intuitively, an infallible " Open Sesame." It was Eve, wander-ing in Eden with nothing to do, save mischief, who first found the weasel asleep, and availed herself of the opportunity to shave off his eye-brows. O Mr. Joseph Charles Parkinson, author of " Under Government;" O communicative writer of " The Master Key to Public Offices ;" O soul-harrowing editor of the " Note-Book of a Private Detective "—you don't know what goes on under crinoline government, or what master keys to private offices our domestic detectives keep hanging to the prettiest of. châtelaines. You never imagine that dear, smiling Mrs. Can-dor was born Mademoiselle Fouché; and that Mrs. Lambkin's first husband was Captain Yarde, from Scotland.

It is better that we should remain in ignorance of the whole extent of espionage that is exercised

over us. If everybody knew what other people
knew about them, this world would be as intolerable as the tigers' den at the Zoological Gardens
in hot weather.

I have said enough, however, it is to be hoped,
to set all the Mrs. Candors and Mrs. Lambkins,
who have anything to learn in their profession,
busy searching Mr. C.'s umbrella and the lining
of Mr. L.'s hat. Pending their anticipated dis-
coveries, I will revert to the charnel-house topic.
It was fortunate for me, on the morning when
those bones came out, that nothing of a more
incriminatory nature had been found upon me.
It is not the season for masquerades ; but I have
known dreadful scenes to arise through the turning up of a crumpled bit of pasteboard covered
with black silk, with two eyeholes and a fringe
of sham lace. A pair of white kid-gloves, too,
when you have left home in dark ones, may lead
to much that is disastrous. A theatrical pass-
check, with "Magenta" or "Hippopotamus"
printed on it, does not look well ; and there are
numerous other things a man may bring home
in his pocket without being aware of them—
circulars from the Church Missionary Society ;
invitations to dine with the Gas and Gaiter Club ;
four sovereigns won at cards, when he left home
with two half-crowns and a fourpenny bit ; tooth-
picks ; programmes of the entertainments at

Cremorne; champagne corks; cribbage-pegs; strange latch-keys; and the like; all of which, unless he have a talent for diplomatic explanation, may bring him into dire trouble.

There was nothing against me on this particular morning save the Bones. To diplomatize I deemed unworthy, and at once made a clean breast of it. You, *lecteur débonnaire*, shall be a party to the confession. I had been to dine at the annual festival of the Acclimatisation Society at St. James's Hall, Piccadilly; I had partaken in moderation of *grenouilles à la poulette*, a fricassee of FROGS in white sauce, which the Society seem to be seeking to acclimatise in our kitchens and on our dinner-tables—for frogs can scarcely be said to be exotic to our marshes and ponds— and which are, I assure you, very nice eating; I had picked a number of frogs' bones clean, and I brought them home as a kind of spoil or trophy, to hang up, in lieu of the dried scalps of my foes, in the domestic wigwam. That is to say, I meant to keep them under a clockcase, where, completely desiccated, carefully perfumed, and tastefully gilt all over, I still preserve the shell of a crawfish which once decorated a *vol au vent à la financière*, and which I keep, not only by reason of its being a charming miniature model of a lobster, but because it serves as a memento of one of the friskiest fish-dinners at

Blackwall at which I ever had the honor of being
an invited guest.

So, the murder is out; and it being difficult
to associate any very flagrant degree of moral
turpitude with the possession of the tibia and
fibula of poor froggee, peace, for an instant disturbed by the unwonted appearance of the Bones,
was soon restored, and I was permitted to expa-
tiate on the peculiarities of a very strange but
very succulent dinner.

The Acclimatisation Society of Great Britain
and Ireland, is composed of a number of ener-
getic and public-spirited men, who do not stick
at trifles.   Approach thee like the rugged Russian bear or the armed rhinoceros, and you won't
frighten a member of the Acclimatisation Society.
He will do his best to acclimatise the bear and
the rhinoceros; and if they are good to eat, he
will devour them *à la croque au sel.*

Reader, I must deprecate any indignant feelings which may arise in your breast, if, in the
course of the next page and a half of this Article,
I make use of a good many words of dubious
French origin.   I shall be compelled to quote
the bill of fare; and as Mr. Donald, of St. James's
Hall, keeps a French *chef,* of course it was but
natural for that functionary to draw up his *menu*
in culinary French.   The Acclimatisation Society
dinner was of a duplex or rather a triplex nature.

It comprised, first, the elements of a first-rate
French banquet; next, those of a substantial
English repast; and thirdly, a variety of abnormal dishes and wines of cosmopolitan extraction
and exceptional character, specially introduced
for the occasion by the Acclimatisation Society.
Thus, we had clear turtle, and *bisque* and *potage
à la Bedford*, and then we were to have had
" white soup of the Channel Islands ;" made of
the conger eel—a creature so despised that the
starving Irish have refused to add flavor and
nutriment to their potatoes by boiling them with
a salted steak of the conger; and yet it is ad-
duced, as a curious illustration of national prejudice, that while starving Paddy rejects the conger,
large quantities of the fish are boiled down into
stock, to be used in the making of turtle-soup in
London. I hope there wasn't any conger eel in
my *tortue claire*.

I strive not to give way to prejudice as to what
I eat or drink, and have swallowed in my time,
not a few "exceptional" viands; but I don't think
I could manage the white soup of the Channel
Islands. It happened after all that the conger-
eel soup did not make its appearance on the din-
ner-table. A jar of it had been sent from Jersey,
but, owing to the heat of the weather, had turned
bad *en route*, and some *potage à la reine* had been
substituted, which looked quite as nasty as the

"white soup" is said to be. I tried hard to eat it, but gave up the attempt at last in despair, mingled with disgust.

I didn't presume to proclaim my aversion to the bilious-looking mess aloud; for the majority of the company present were "swells" of the very heaviest fashionable or scientific order; but the facetious Mr. Bernal Osborne, behind whom I had the honor to sit, felt no such scruples. It happened that the Duke of Newcastle, who had been announced to take the chair, couldn't come. He had been asked to tea I believe, by royalty, at Kew; and at the fifty-ninth minute Mr. Herman Merivale, C. B., was elected to the presidency. But Mr. Osborne accounted for his grace's absence in quite another manner. He pointed out that the Duke had taken the chair at the Acclimatisation banquet in the previous year; that he had been tempted to try the potage of conger eels; that he hadn't quite recovered from the effects thereof; and that he had stayed away from this year's dinner through a wholesome fear of being once more compelled to swallow a plateful of the abhorred white soup of the Channel Islands. The audience roared with laughter at this humorous hypothesis; only the fact of the soup not being of conger eel at all, which afterwards oozed out, somewhat detracted from the force of Mr. Osborne's sarcasm.

And yet, eels are savory things. Fried, they are delicious; spatch-cocked, they are glorious; and stewed—ah! no more on that exciting topic. When the Old Serpent appears in the guise of a stewed eel, it is impossible to resist him. (Then, again, as a soup there was *bouillabaisse*. Now there are a great many would-be epicures who profess to delight in this curious *souché* of fish, spice, and garlic, because Mr. Thackeray has written upon it one of the most beautiful lyrics extant in any language.] When your young University man first goes to Paris, he is sure to inquire after "the new street of the little fields," and his soul thirsts after a mess of *bouillabaisse* and the "Chambertin with yellow seal." For the Chambertin, *ça me va ;* but as regards the *bouillabaisse*, I would rather take something "exceptional" in the way of *potage colimaçon* or *tripes à la mode de Caen.* It may stand high in the Provençale cuisine; it may be the favorite fish-stew of the Bay of Biscay—imagine the ship-wrecked mariners :—

> " There they lay
> All that day
> (Devouring *bouillabaisse*) in the Bay of Biscay, oh !"

but it is nevertheless horribly nauseous. The culinary sages of the Acclimatisation Society tell us that "it is made of various fishes, but its

11

indispensable ingredients are red mullet, tomatoes, red pepper, red burgundy, oil, and garlic. Soles, gurnets, dories, and whitings are admissible into this dish." Yes, and there is another item admissible : but on which I fancy the Acclimatisation Society, were they aware of it, would scarcely care to dwell.

At Marseilles, where *bouillabaisse* is made in perfection, the cook always has at his side a caldron of *boiling tallow*—tallow, not oil, mind! He plunges a long rolling-pin into this caldron, withdraws it, and holds it aloft till the tallow is congealed. Then he gives it another dip, and another and another, until the rolling-pin is surrounded by a sufficient thickness of solidified tallow. And then he plunges the greasy staff into the kettle of *bouillabaisse* and turns it round and round till all the tallow is melted from it, and has become incorporated with the delightful *pot-pourri* of " red mullet, tomatoes, red pepper, red burgundy, oil, and garlic." After this, go and eat your fill of *bouillabaisse*.

Against fish-soups, however, I raise no voice. Turtle, terrapin, oyster, *bisque*, are all exquisite. The Italians, again, have their *zuppa marinana*, which is not (saving the presence of the A. S.) at all like *bouillabaisse;* and the Russians make a very appetising piscine pottage (when you are acclimatised to it) called *batwinia*. The stock of this is composed of *kvas*, or half-brewed barley-beer and oil, and into this is put the fish known as the *sterlet* of the Volga, or the *sassina* of the Gulf of Finland, together with bay-leaves, pepper, and lumps of ice. I will match *batwinia* any day against *bouillabaisse*.

So much for soups. Now for the fish proper. Salmon *à la Duchesse de Sutherland*, turbot stuffed *à la Hollandaise*, do not call for particular remark. *Blanchaille*, I apprehend, is French for whitebait; and if that fish exist in France, or if whitebait be a real fish at all, and not an artful combination of batter, pepper, and currants thrown in to serve as eyes, I will bow to Mr. Donald's *chef*. "Caller salmon" was put forward as "exceptional," the peculiarity of the dish being that the salmon has been boiled as soon as possible after being taken from the water, so that the fat has curded between the flanks. I hope the zeal of the A. S. won't lead them to the discovery that the adipose matter in salmon may be curded even more rapidly by boiling the fish alive.

We have heard quite enough about crimped cod; and after watching the evolutions of that noble, blue-black, armor-plated man-of-war in the vivarium at the Zoological Gardens, one almost feels inclined to recommend the practice of boiling lobsters alive to the notice of the

secretary of the Royal Society for the Prevention
of Cruelty to Animals. If " the cardinal of the
seas," as Jules Janin, with amusingly blundering
humor, called him, could only be born red, what
an immensity of agony he might save himself, to
be sure !

"Charr" was served fresh. It is usually
served potted, and is a capital " pick up " if you
are breakfasting in bed, and feel faint. It may
vie as a restorative with dried cod-sounds.
Caviar they gave us not; yet to relish this
delightful conserve of sturgeon I think the
British public stand sadly in need of being acclimatised.

We see the neat little kegs of caviar in
Morel's or Fortnum and Mason's windows; but
only enthusiastic epicures think of buying them.
To acclimatise yourself to caviar, you should
begin on a course of Dutch herrings washed
down by a couple of tumblers (taken fasting) of
cod-liver oil. After that, empty a pot of black-
currant jam into a salt-cellar, and cram the
amalgamated contents into a sardine-box half
full of fish. Stir well, and keep the box in a
warm room for a fortnight. Then serve on
bread-and-butter, and tell me how you like it.
The mixture as before (with perhaps a little of
Warren's blacking added) is very like caviar. In
Mahomet's seventh heaven the houris always eat

a pound and a half of it for breakfast on Tuesdays and Fridays.

"Lucioperca" is the pike-perch found throughout Northern Europe. "Although excellent for the purposes of the table," writes the Apicius of the A. S., its voracity is such that its introduction into this country is not recommended, except in ponds especially devoted to its propagation." In these special ponds, I suppose, the lucioperca would eat one another, until the sole survivor of the tontine assumed the dimensions of a whale.

There were no sea-slugs this year, and there was no bird's-nest soup: but there was plenty of sturgeon, which reminds you of a tough veal-cutlet sent for his misdemeanors on board ship and returned with a fishy flavor. I missed kangaroo-steamer also, and gambo-soup: nor, so far as I could ascertain, was there any parrot-pie on the table. The *entrées*, however, were very rich and varied. The *suprémes de volaille* cockscombed or truffled, the *croustades* of quails, the cutlets and curries and *kromeskis* and sweetbreads, I dismiss at once. They belong to Mr. Donald, not to the Society. In the "exceptional" domain we had pepper-pot, that wondrous West-Indian dish, that salmagundi of fowl, beef, and mutton, peppered up to the maintruck, and sauced with the cassareep or inspissated juice of

the manioc root; the whole kept simmering and
seething in a huge jar or pipkin. I consumed
vast quantities of pepper-pot. Dear old mess!
I felt to the manner born of it; it was my *pot au
feu.*

Shall an Irishman not love his praties, a
Scotchman his oatmeal-porridge? I was weaned
on pepper-pot and mangoes. The taste of the
cassareep brought floating before my mind
memories of the dead and gone past; preserved
ginger and guava jelly, yams and plantains,
tamarinds and arrowroot, banyans and pig-galls,
and grinning servants with black faces and yellow kerchiefs twisted round their woolly pates.
And yet I was never in the West Indies in my
life.

Some "Pallas sand-grouse" proved very toothsome. These are the birds whose recent visits
to this country have given the chatty-correspon-
dents of "The Field" so capital an opportunity for
displaying their acumen, and whose dusky selves
are among the chief attractions of those charming
Sunday afternoons when the British aristocracy
are pleased to disport themselves at the Zoo. I
didn't eat any of the poultry introduced with the
fantastic title of *poulets à l'émancipation des
négres;* but I heard them very well spoken of.
"The peculiarity of this fowl," I quote Apicius,
or J. L., Esq., " is, that the skin and periosteum

are quite black, but the flesh is perfectly white."
Mr. Tegetmeier, of the Philoperisteron Society,
says that it is the *coq négre* of Tammerick, and
must not be confounded with the small silky
bantam known as the *coq à duvet*.

But I am in a hurry to get to the *grosses pièces*.
Haunch of venison, saddle of mutton—we know
all about these; but what think you of *agneau
chinois rôti entier, farci aux pistaches, servi au
pilaff et couscoussou!*—a Chinese lamb roasted
whole, stuffed with pistachio-nuts and served
with couscoussou, which last is a preparation of
wheat used among the Moors, Algerines, and
other natives of the North-African littoral, in
place of rice. I have heard that the Moorish
young ladies are fattened for the matrimonial
market by a diet *ad libitum* of this strengthening
compound.

The couscoussou is made into balls and stuffed
into the mouth of the marriageable young lady,
till she grows as tired of balls as a belle who has
been through three seasons of quadrilles and
polkas without getting a single offer. If the
damsel won't eat any more couscoussou, they
administer the bastinado till she feels hungry
again. They do such odd things in Barbary!

Well, how about the education of goose-livers
with a view to *pâté de foie gras?* How about
stuffing turkeys? and don't we send our sons

to a crammer when we are anxious that they should obtain a Government clerkship or a direct commission ?

"In the lamb roasted whole," says Apicius (or J. L., Esq.), "we have one of the earliest dishes on record in the history of cookery. Stuffed with pistachio-nuts and served with pilaff, it at the same time illustrates the antiquity of the art, and gives an example of the food upon which millions of our fellow-creatures are sustained. The lamb proves the excellent flavor of the Ong-Ti breed of Chinese sheep, the introduction of which is one of the special objects of this society.

Thus far Apicius; but I take the liberty of stating that I should prefer Ong-Ti mutton to Ong-Ti lamb. The Chinese lamb was decidedly flabby, and, as is usually the case when an animal is cooked entire, the fire had burnt up one part and left the others nearly raw. The carver did not love or fear me sufficiently to give me a liberal allowance of pistachio, and the pilaff stood in need of a little *ghee* or fluid butter (rancid, if you please) being poured over it. However, it was a noble experiment, and shows that the society are disposed to adopt no half-measures.

"Fawn of fallow deer," "ribs of beef between buffalo and Kerry cow"—these were *pièces de résistance* whose presence only I am enabled to

record. "Their names," says J. L. Apicius, Esq.,
pithily, "explain their intention." There was a
red-deer ham, and one of bear—very succulent;
but why couldn't the society have made an
arrangement with an enterprising hair-dresser,
and caused "another fine bear" to be slaughtered,
in order that the company might taste a bear-
steak and a tender sirloin? I ate bear once at
a Russian dinner-party (where it was introduced,
I admit, as a curiosity, and not as an ordinary
dish), and a half-a-dozen mouthfuls made me sick
for a fortnight afterwards. The meat was tough,
glutinous, and had, besides, a dreadful, half-
aromatic, half-putrescent flavor, as though it had
first been rubbed with asafœtida and then hung
up for a month in Mr. Rimmel's shop.

Bison tongues, Chinese yam, Bayonne ham, I
dismiss; but was disappointed at not seeing on the
table any of the famous donkey-flesh sausages of
Bologna. A roast monkey, too (most delicious
eating when stuffed with chestnuts), was a desi-
deratum; and I asked in vain for rat. Snails,
too, were absent; but *en revanche* I took my fill
of frogs.

When you were a little boy at school, you
probably ate a good many frogs. Our practice
was, when we had caught them, to pinch our
nostrils with the fingers of one hand, and holding
the dapper little froggee lightly with the other,

11*

to allow him to jump down our throats. There was a tradition among us that to swallow live frogs (for the process could not be called eating) made a boy strong and valorous, and almost un-sentient to the cuts of the cane. As we advanced in years we took a distaste for frogs. We were patriots. We grew to hate frogs because we heard that the French liked them and that they formed a principal item in the diet of that viva-cious and ingenious people. The truth is, how-ever, that frogs are regarded in France as a most luxurious delicacy, and are correspondingly ex-pensive. The Marché St. Honoré is the most usual place for their vendition; and as only the hind-legs are eaten by the Parisians, and the price is seldom under fifteen francs a dozen, a dish of frogs is only seen at the table of a million-aire. Of their tenderness, succulence, and deli-cacy of flavor, there can be no question.

The *grenouilles à la poulette* at the Acclima-tisation dinner were superb. The white sauce left nothing to be desired. I ate as much frog as ever I could get; and, as related above, I brought the bones home in my waistcoat-pocket as a trophy of victory over a stupid and irrational pre-judice. We eat the dirty pig, the dirtier duck, and yet we turn up our noses at the clean-living, and clean-feeding frog. Had not the Acclima-tisation Society a hundred other claims to public support, our gratitude would be due to them for thus bravely teaching Englishmen to eat frogs.

This Homeric, this Apician, this Vitellian, this Gargantuan banquet—the like of which I never saw before, but fondly hope to see again—was washed down by copious streams of Sherry, Hock, Meursault (very good), Red Burgundy, Champagne, and Moselle.

Among exceptional wines we had a whole host of Greek ones. Santorin we quaffed, and Thera, and St. Elie, and Corinth, and Mount Hymettus, Vi Santo, Cyprus, and Lacrima Cristi; while from the Magyar vineyards came Muscat, Badasconyer, Dioszeger Bakatar, Hock, Ruszte, Szamarodny, Adlerberger Ofner, and Tokay. Among the Greeks, my humble verdict is recorded in favor of St. Elie. The Hungarian are stout wines, of a swashbuckling flavor; but a man needs a strong head to drink pottle deep of them.

Such was the dinner to which I came a little late, and whence I brought away the Bones. *Tardè venientibus, ossa.* I laughed as well as I could for eating and drinking strange things all the evening.

The room was very hot, and crammed besides with nearly all the notabilities of the day; but the feast was so rich and so rare that we should have cheerfully partaken of it even in a Turkish bath. There were but few drawbacks to the entertainment.

The chairman, it is true, talked Colonial Office
and "Quarterly Review" in a torrent of fluent
platitudes, till I ran my eye down the bill of fare
to see if *red tape au naturel* wasn't included in
the removes; but we were not there for the purpose of listening to speechifying.

The "exceptional" dishes had deprived the
waiters of the few wits conferred on them by nature; and one or two of their body appeared to
have been partaking surreptitiously of white soup
of the Channel Islands until the decomposed conger eel had got into their heads. The ostrich
eggs, again, were not forthcoming, to the bitter
disappointment of Mr. Bernal Osborne; and
there was no horse. Almost everything else,
however, in the way of edible or potable rarity
was to be found on the table; and I believe that,
had those latest lions of London, the Maori chiefs,
been among the guests, the Council of the Society would have revolved, at least, the expe-
diency of serving up a cold boiled missionary,
with a stewed baby and a baked young woman
to follow, as a delicate attention to the distinguished New Zealanders.

They were not there, however; nor, unfortu
nately, was another gentleman, whose absence
was most sincerely to be deplored, not only for
our sakes, but for his own.

The joint secretaries to the Acclimatisation
Society are Messrs. Frank Buckland, the dis

tinguished naturalist and promoter of pisciculture, and James Lowe, who in a gastronomical tournament would cheerfully give the ghost of Brillat-Savarin twenty, and with his arms tied behind his back, defeat Dr. Kitchener, Prince Cambacérès, and Mr. Hayward. At the last moment Mr. Lowe was attacked by sudden illness, and his attendance at the banquet was compulsorily foregone. It was a heavy blow for everybody, including Mr. Lowe. But such is life.

ON A YOUNG LADY IN A BALCONY.

A DISTINGUISHED English writer has been occupied, I am informed, for some years in the composition of a book with the seductive title of the
"Footsteps of Luther." My acquaintance with
contemporary literature is of so limited a nature,
and I know so little of what is going on in the
great world, that it is quite possible that the book
I speak of may have been completed, published,
and reviewed these six months past, and that its
gifted author has been long since crowned with
laurel or overwhelmed with abuse: the terms being, to many intents and purposes, synonymous.
If this be indeed the case, I am sure I beg the
author's pardon very humbly. I know that he
went to Germany to write the book, and took a
camera and a quantity of collodion with him to
photograph the footprints of the Great Reformer
as he wandered; but here my positive information ceases.

My only object in alluding to the "Footsteps
of Luther" was to point out that, good as that
title was, it seemed to me that I knew of a better.

In Protestant England, of course, every tittle of
information having even the remotest connection
with mighty Doctor Martin is interesting, and,
after a kind, sacred; but at Geneva, it may be,
the Sire Jean Chauvin, otherwise Calvin, is first
favorite in the Reforming heart; and if we go
southwards, and across certain mountains, we
shall find many millions of religionists who wick-
edly maintain that, if Martin Luther could have
been made, by persuasion of the secular arm, to
dance upon nothing, such aërial footsteps would
have been the gratefullest to the Church at large.
But here is a book whose title, were it faithfully
and skilfully borne out by its matter, would
be sure to please all, and could offend none.
What do you think of "The Footsteps in Italy of
William Shakespeare?"   Can you imagine a
tome more delightful?   Once, when I was young
and hale, and my heart fat as butter with conceit, I thought of sitting down to write such a
book myself.   It was years and years ago—before I had been set face to face with my own
ignorance, and, glancing in the glass of experience, had found how very long my ears were.
I remember that I propounded my design in the
boxes of the Porte St. Martin Theatre in Paris
(where they were playing Alexandre Dumas's
"Orestie") to a great English man of letters.
The illustrious personage saw my drift at once,

and deigned to say to me, "I envy you your subject." *Il l'a bien dit*, he who never envied mortal man, but ever strove to help and to encourage the weakest and the dullest, and to give frank praise to his few compeers. Well, I never grappled with the subject that he professed to envy me. I did not forget, I simply neglected it. I have been haunted by this abandoned one many a time. Here it is still, an embryo crying for maturity; a blossom that, were I worthy, would have given place, ere now, to ripe and luscious fruit. However, it is now too late; so, to preserve my bantling from atrophy (here is a fine confusion of metaphors at your service!) I desert it on a doorstep. With averted face, and tearful eye, and remorseful heart, I place it in the turning-cradle. May some good Sister of Charity receive, to cherish it; and may it find better fortune in the Foundling Hospital for Wit than in my brains!

Only last night (I remember now, as I Breakfast for thè last time in Bed), sitting in the stalls of the Princess's Theatre, and witnessing the tragedy of "Romeo and Juliet," the image of my abortive book came across me, and I longed to find some man or woman of wit and parts who would turn my vision into reality. For I should be loth to see the task undertaken by one of the common herd of scribblers. Naturally, now that the notion is common property, every botcher has a right to try his 'prentice hand upon it. Hircius probably will swear that he thought ten years ago of following Shakespeare up and down Italy; and Spungius may endeavor to raise money on account from the booksellers on the security of the idea. But to do the thing thoroughly, a host of rare qualities would be needed. M. d'Alembert once dotted down a few of the acquirements which, in his opinion (and D'Alembert knew a thing or two), were requisite to a writer who aspired to be a Biblical critic. The dottings-down filled half a dozen closely-printed pages; the which I respectfully commend (together with Voltaire's "Défense de mon Oncle," and Bayle's second "Life of David") to the attention of the Right Reverend Father in Mumbo Jumbo, Dr. Colenso. He will find that there were some strong men before Agamemnon, and some hard nuts, which stronger men than he essayed to crack before the demolition of the authenticity of the Pentateuch became as fashionable an amusement as rubbing one's nose against Zadkiel's crystal ball, or going to see Blondin on the high rope.

He who would write the "Footsteps in Italy of William Shakespeare" (I thought in my, stall, should be, first, a copious and profound Shakesperian scholar, and an acute Shakesperian critic. He should know the plays by heart; have the poems on the tip of his tongue; and harbor some tangible hypothesis on the sonnets. He should be well up in his Hazlitt, his Schlegel, his Maginis, his Coleridge, his Dyce, his Staunton, and his Halliwell. All that Malone and Steevens have written should be familiar to him. Then he should be a linguist, who had read through Guicciardini without being daunted at the War of Pisa, and mastered all the Foreign State-Papers in our Record Office (unhappy Turnbull!) and all the Relations of the Venetian Ambassadors lately disentombed by M. Armand Baschet from the Convent of the Frari. Furthermore, he should be an artist, practised in the various styles of Turner and Calcott, of Stanfield and Holland. In addition, he should be a polished, patient, appreciative, and observant traveller; a Rogers, a Lear, a Eustace, a Kinglake, a Canon Wordsworth. Finally, he should bring to his Italian journeyings the mordant humor of Heinrich Heine, the metaphysical sentiment of George Sand, the voluptuous word-painting of Byron, the minute pencilling of the President de Brosses. Finally, he should be a gentleman. Armed *cap-à-pie* with all these qualities, and with plenty of money, time, industry, and health, and sufficient reticence to burn his MS., sheet by sheet, if it proved faulty, he might in the end produce, I think, such a work as would infinitely delight this generation, and one that posterity would not willingly let die.

I don't think it militates in the slightest degree against the value of my ideal book to be told that Shakespeare never was in Italy. He had been everywhere, as he was everything, in the spirit. The people who cudgel their brains as to his medical knowledge and his legal knowledge—as to whether he was ever a scrivener or an apothecary, a soldier or a sailor, a butcher or a horse-couper—are, to my mind, donkeys, and nothing more. He was a clairvoyant. His Elsinore is in the very Denmark; his Dunsinane in Scotland; his forests near Athens; his Cliff in Kent; his Belmont in Venetia (I have seen Portia's house; it is on the Banks of the Brenta, and is now inhabited by an enriched *prima donna*); his "park and palace in Navarre" in the Basque country; not necessarily because he ever actually or corporeally journeyed to those places, but because the Almighty had gifted him with the power of seeing things in his soul, and of describing them in matchless music. And in the main, though all his absolute peregrinations may have extended no further than between London and Stratford, and the suburbs of the metropolis, he is a more trustworthy traveller than Mandeville or Purchas, Hackluyt or Marco Polo.

In the whole Shakesperian catalogue there is no play more thoroughly Italian than " Romeo and Juliet." Enthusiasm for the mighty master may be the parent of such an opinion, you may surmise; but just take a through ticket by the Victor Emmanuel Railway, and leave the train at the Porta Nuova, Verona, and trot on the next day to Mantua, and you will come to be of my mind. Gorgeous as are Mr. John Gilbert's illustrations to the Routledge edition, his superb designs, when he touches the Italian dramas, seem to me meagre and shrivelled. It is in the text that you must look for the genuine local coloring, the choice Italian. There you will feel the real Italian sunshine, the balmy nights, the bath of moonlight, the lounging, lazy lives of the men and women, the saunterings and sighings and whisperings, chequered every now and then by fierce outbreaks of passion—by the sharp scream, the torrent of passionate invective, the quick curse, the sudden stab. Upon my word, not six weeks since at Verona I saw *Sampson* biting his thumb at *Abram*, and *Gregory* backing him up; and then there was a *rixe*, and the Capulet women rushed out of their houses and slapped the *Montague* children violently; and *Benvolio* strove in vain to quell the turmoil, and old *Capulet* in his gown (he carried on the profession of a money-changer, and had been disturbed from his *siesta*) came shuffling out of his shop, with *Lady Capulet*, in a dingy bed-gown, clinging to him ; and then the venerable *Montague* (who had subsided into the peaceful pursuit of vending saffron-tinted sausages) issued from his back parlor, accompanied by *his* lady, and gave *Capulet* a piece of his mind; and then the women scolded, and the men stormed, and the dogs barked, and everybody bit his or her thumb, or snapped their fingers at everybody else; and people who had seemingly nothing on earth to do with the fray, flung open third-floor casements, and joined with shrill verbiage in it; and there was, on the whole, a devil of a commotion. It did not concern me ; but I felt so excited, that had I had a weapon on my thigh, I am afraid I should have drawn, and had a lunge at somebody. As it was, I found myself in fierce parley with an old woman who sold lemonade under an archway; and where it would have ended I know not, had not, in the nick of time, *Prince Escalus* (represented for the nonce by an Austrian corporal's guard with fixed bayonets) come up, and abused the combatants all round in Teutonic Italian. Some one—I believe *Gregory*—was marched off to the guard-house ; and I made my peace with the old lady who sold lemonade; and *Capulet* went back to his *siesta*, and *Montague* to his sausages. But until I left Verona by the

Porta Vescova, I was in a perpetual day-dream
about "Romeo and Juliet." Wherever the road
bifurcated, I expected to meet the fiery *Tybalt*,
his sword drawn, raging up one thoroughfare, in
search of the pacific *Benvolis* (an Italian quaker
he) who was quietly trotting down another.
What a man of men he was, that *Tybalt!*
Shakespeare knew well enough that he would be
possible nowhere but in Italy; so he put him in
Verona. The heat of the climate made him mad.
His sword turned red-hot in its scabbard, and
burnt through the leather, and scorched his
thigh. Then he went at it, hammer and tongs:

> "Non schirar, non parar, non ritirarsi
> Voglion costor, nè qui destrezza ha parte;
> Non danno i colpi, or finti, or pieni, or scarsi;
> Toglie l' ira e 'l furor l' uso dell' arte.
> Odi le spade orribilmente urtarsi
> A mezzo il ferro! Il piè d' orma non parte:
> Sempre è il piè fermo, e la man sempre in moto;
> Nè scende taglio in van, nè punto a voto." *

Here is the real *Tybalt* for you, when he has
gotten an antagonist worthy of his blood-lustful

---

* "They wish neither to avoid the combat, to parry the
blows, nor to fly. Skill hath no part in the conflict; their
thrusts are no make-believes: now straightforward, now oblique.
Rage and hatred rob them of the resources of art. Here the
horrible shock of their swords clashing together! Their feet
are firm and motionless; their hands always on the move.
Not a blow is given in vain; not a thrust is lost."

steel. He is a good swordsman; but in his craze for killing, he despises carte and tierce and reason demonstrative. Here is *Tybalt* foaming at the mouth, blind with fury, hacking, hewing, slashing, stabbing away. Surely Shakespeare must have read these burning lines of the old Italian poet, and conjured up the fiery *Tybalt* from the ringing rhyme. That " *Odi le spade orribilmente urtarsi a mezzo il ferro !*" was amply sufficient for the clairvoyant. And indeed I am, in this surmise, not winnowing the wind; for there is every likelihood that William Shakespeare did read the lines I have transcribed. They are quoted by Montaigne, and Montaigne's Essays were, we know, from an undoubted autograph, among the favorite reading of our poet.

I never heard a burst of laughter from a *caffè* that afternoon in Verona without peeping in to see the gallant *Mercutio* swinging his legs on a marble table, and bantering the love-lorn *Romeo* sighing over his sugar-and-water. I went to see the so-called tomb of the ill-starred lovers; but that apocryphal monument did not help my illusion. The streets were enough for me. What does it matter, I asked myself, whence the master obtained his plot, or who the lovers really were; whether, as Mr. Douce essayed to prove, the original tale comes from a Greek author, one Xenophon Ephesius; or whether the events recorded took place, not at Verona, but at Sienna, *Romeo* being "a young man of good family, named Mariotti Mignaletti," and *Juliet* a certain Donna Gianozza? All these are trifles. Whether the romance was of Luigi da Porto's making, or of Bandello's, or of Boisteau's, thence translated by Arthur Brooke, frets me little. It is enough that Shakespeare, from a lovely legend, was permitted to make an immortal drama: that he has laid the scene in Italy; and that the play is Italian to the very core.

In what part of the continent if you please, save Italy, would that garden-scene have been feasible? Italy is the country where, after the scorching day, comes a cool but temperate night. Italy is the land where young people sit up all night to make love, and where, too, they do tumble into love with one another at first sight. In decorous England, *Juliet's* sudden passion for *Romeo* might have been considered improper. In Italy, nothing could be more natural. It is where the sun is so warm that the corn ripens so quickly. And the impromptu masquerade; and the pretty fib told by *Juliet* that she was going out to confession, when she is bent on being married! In England, a young lady would have told her mamma that she was going to Mudie's or to Regent Street to purchase two yards and a half of maize-colored ribbon. And then the changes of scene, the frequent dialogues that take place " in a street," " another street," " a public place !" Italy is the country above all others where people meet in streets and public places to talk together by the hour, to chat, to .gossip, to flirt, and to quarrel; for those streets and places, you see, are lined with cool and shady arcades, along whose pavements you can saunter, against whose pillars you can lean, free from dust, or heat, or jostling crowds.

But farewell, fair Verona, and Heaven deliver thee speedily from the Austrian corporal's guard and the dominion of the double-headed eagle generally! I must not forget that I am in Oxford Street, and in the stalls of an English playhouse, and that my business to-night is only, by implication, with " the footsteps in Italy of William Shakespeare," but more directly with Mademoiselle Stella Colas, from the Imperial French Theatre at St. Petersburg, who under-takes the part of *Juliet*, and, thorough French-woman as she is, plays it in English.

The pretty creature! Mademoiselle Stelle Colas is by this time gone back to St. Petersburg, and the praise or blame I am presumptuous enough to mete out to her will probably never reach her ears, unless indeed the editor of the "Nevsky Magazine" chooses to transfer this article (to which he is very welcome) to the next number of his publication. Nor, perhaps, were this "Breakfast in Bed" brought under the notice of the charming Stella, would she be much the wiser for it ; for I have heard spiteful people on this side of the water hint that her acquaintance with the English vernacular was of the most limited nature, and that she mastered the speeches set down for *Capulet's* hapless daughter mainly in the poll-parrot fashion. 'Tis no disgrace for a French *tragédienne* to have done so. Have we not all been told that the illustrious Rachel herself was not gifted with the faculty of understanding much of the purport of the lines she spoke, all native as the language was to her; that, word by word, and syllable by syllable, the couplets had to be laboriously drummed into her, until she was in a position to *débiter la tirade*, to roll forth her lava stream of declamation ; and that those wonderful movements and bits of by-play—few in number, certainly, and somewhat monotonous—which used to excite our amazement and admiration were all taught her, in the purest mechanical manner, by her instructor, Monsieur Sanson? Rachel did not care much as to what author she recited from ; Racine, Corneille, Molière, Ducis, or Légouvé, were all the same to her. She had something in her—wonderful, Heaven-given genius ; but it lay deep, dormant; it wanted smelting; the gold needed to be separated from the ore; and it was for Monsieur Sanson to use the divining rod and the digger's cradle. The English actor—perhaps Mr. John Ryder?—whose pleasant task it was to "coach" Stella Colas had not, perhaps, so difficult a labor. This fascinating young woman was evidently highly appreciative amd imaginative, and probably seized the scope and meaning of *Juliet's* character long ere she understood the half of Shakespeare's words. I question whether, after all, she had anything beyond a vaguely general comprehension of them.

The pretty creature! I say again. Was there ever such a darling *Juliet?* Lest I should be accused of impertinent personality in thus publicly expressing my admiration for a pretty girl, let it be understood that my compliments are addressed not to her, but to the series of *cartes de visite* published towards the close of her engagement. Her photographs were well-nigh as pretty as herself. Such childish innocence; such langorous love of the handsome *Montague* with the green-silk legs; such winning fondness for the nurse who scolded but idolized her; such affectionate reverence for her harsh papa and mamma; such trust and confidence in *Friar Lawrence;* such sweet and simple womanly daintinesses, were probably never developed by the camera before.

And here let me be permitted a slight digression. To us English people of the nineteeth century, the behavior of *Capulet* and his wife to their daughter, can scarcely fail to appear barbarous and unnatural. We have match-making mammas in our midst, no doubt, who lead their daughters a terrible life on vexed questions of matrimonial alliance; and ill-natured papas, who threaten to cut their girls off with a shilling if they don't immediately discard the penniless captain for the rich cotton spinner. But the *Capulets* in modern life are, I hope, extinct ; or, if they are to be found lurking in odd nooks and corners, they must be set down as monstrosities. Take yourself back to medieval Italy, however, and *Juliet's* papa and mamma become the most natural people in the world. The old Italian novels and chronicles are full of Lord and Lady *Capulets*. If we glance at a recent, to say little of the present, state of French society, we shall find parental harshness carried to an extent scarcely less hideous. Do you remember *Ginevra*, the heroine of Honoré de Balzac's most pathetic romance? *Ginevra* is only *Juliet*. Her vindictive Corsican parents are only *Capulets ;* the man she persists in marrying is simply a *Montague*. "Marry the *County Paris*, or get thee to a nunnery." "Marry the *County Paris*, or be turned out of doors." "Do as you are bidden, or be locked up in the coal-cellar on bread-and-water." "Choose your bridal dress, or never see your papa and mamma's face again." These were the agreeable refrains of the family ditty.

I am afraid that, if we turned away from Italy and directed our glance towards England, we should find enough of parental cruelty and to spare, not only in Shakespeare's time, but for a hundred and fifty years afterwards. In one of Cibber's comedies, a young married lady, say *Berinthia*, asks another youthful matron, say *Clarissa* (who detests her husband), why she did not marry the man of her choice. "My mother would have whipped me," answers *Clarissa* simply. And Materfamilias *would* have whipped her, too, soundly. The story of Dr. Johnson and the young ladies in Lincolnshire might be quoted in confirmation; likewise old Aubrey's garrulous account of things as they were in his youth (close upon Shakespeare's time), when mothers corrected their daughters with their fans—the handle at least half a yard long—and " in the days of their besom discipline used to slash their daughters when they were perfect women." In the great case of the Reverend Mr. Crofton, a Puritan divine, who was prosecuted for barbarously beating his servant-girl, he was asked why he had not used a wand or cane for the purpose of chastisement; whereupon his reverence replied that " his mother, once beating her maid with a wand, *did chance to strike out her eye*, which caused him thenceforth to mislike such usage." A pretty state of things; but our great-great-grandmothers were nevertheless subject to it. Hear Aubrey again: " The gentry and citizens had little learning of any kind, and their way of breeding up their children was suit-able to the rest. They were as severe to their children as their schoolmasters, and their schoolmasters as masters of the House of Correction. The child perfectly loathed the sight of his parents, as the slave his torture. Gentlemen of thirty and forty years old were to stand like mutes and fools bareheaded before their parents; and the daughters (grown women), were to stand at the cupboard-side during the whole time of the proud mother's visit, unless (as the fashion was) leave was desired, forsooth, that a cushion should be given them to kneel upon, brought by the serving-man, after they had done sufficient penance in standing." Ah, the grand old days of authority and discipline! There is a " court cupboard " mentioned in "Romeo and Juliet," and it was doubtless by this " cupboard-side " that poor *Juliet* stood when it pleased her "proud mother" to visit her.

With this you may compare Lady Jane Grey's account of her early tribulations, and her nippings and pinchings in the Suffolk family; but to my mind the clearest gloss on the *Capulets'* usage of their daughter is to be found in the undeniably old ballad of "Willikins and his Dinah," revived in our time with such brilliant success as a comic song by Mr. Robson:

> "As Dinah was a walkin' in the garden one day,
> She met with her father, who to her did say,
>> 'Right tooral, right tooral,' etc.
>
> 'Go! Dinah, go dress yourself in gorgeous array,
> For I've met with a young man so pleasant and gay;
> I've met with a young man of ten thousand a year,
> And he says that he'll make you his love and his dear.
>> 'Right tooral, right tooral,' " etc.

You know how Dinah pleads her youth, and that "to marry that moment she's not much inclined;" and how her "stern parient" flies into a passion, and threatens to leave his large fortune to the nearest of kin; whereupon Dinah commits suicide, and Willikins *felo de se*. You may object that all this is but an after parody of Shakespeare's tragedy, "cup of cold pison" included; but I hold the "London Liquor Merchant," from which Mr. Robson's comic ditty was derived, to be at least as old as "Barbara Allen" and the

"Bailiff's Daughter of Islington," and if not
contemporary with, anterior to, Shakespeare's
age. Both the ballad and the play are indignant protests against paternal harshness; and
there may be some truth in the tradition that
Shakespeare was incited by Lords Essex and
Southampton to bend his wonderful genius to
the embodiment of such a protest on the stage;
to call down public indignation on a Draconic
domestic code imported from abroad, and which,
if we are to believe the memoirs of Silvio Pellico,
existed in Italian households so late as the beginning of the present century.

And I have kept poor dear Stella Colas waiting all this time! Well, with fifteen hundred
admirers, at the very least, watching her every
movement, and applauding her to the very echo,
she can well afford to spare my oblique gaze.
Did I like the French *Juliet?* Did I prefer her
to Fanny Kemble, to Ellen Tree, Helen Faucit?
Well, she was very, very pretty. She dressed in
excellent taste. She had one of the most sensible, polished, and gentlemanlike *Romeos* I ever
desired to see—Mr. Walter Montgomery—who,
on his part, had a wonderful *Apothecary* in Mr.
Belmore. She had an admirable *Friar Lawrence* in Mr. Henry Marston, one of the best
actors on the English stage. And what else?
Well, if the truth must out, I should have liked

to witness Mademoiselle Stella Colas' impersonation of *Juliet* with a ball of cotton securely stuffed into each of my ears. Her pantomime was marvellous. She was full of grace, agility, intelligence, fascination; but I do not like to hear the words of Shakespeare murdered; and that she did so murder them—murdering even while she smiled—is a certainty. In this I may be hypercritical. Foreign tragedians, male and female, on the English boards have become the fashion. We have had a High-Dutch *Hamlet.* We have now had a French *Juliet.* I live in hopes of seeing a Spanish *Ophelia,* and a Cochin-Chinese *Lady Macbeth.*

Of Mademoiselle Stella Colas' astounding intensity of passionate grief, the critics have discoursed until they have become well-nigh as hoarse as the pretty French actress at the end of her screeds of woe. Said a very clever and a very witty lady, who sat by my side in the stalls, to me,

" Of what does that last agony of anguish remind you ?"

" Of Niobe, of Rachel, of Sappho, of the Pythoness, of Madge Wildfire," I answered, heedlessly.

" Not at all," pursued my interlocutor. " *Vous n'y êtes pas! Does not that appalling lament remind you, somehow, of a cat upon the tiles ?*"

The lady was not an Englishwoman; and abroad, as you may know, it is the custom to call things by their names.

But she *was* a pretty creature. Oh! she was fair. I hope she filled Mr. George Vining's treasury to overflowing.. I hope she will marry a Russian Grand-Duke at the very least; and when next Mr. Walter Montgomery plays *Romeo*, I trust he will be enabled to find another *Juliet* as comely and as graceful as Stella Colas. But I very much doubt it.

Lo! I hear the clatter of the crockery-ware on the stairs; and, for the last time, Crazy Jane brings me up my "Breakfast in Bed." For twelve months I have partaken of my morning meal on my back, and feebly philosophized between the sheets. But the year is out. I have grown to acknowledge that my lie-a-bed habits are highly deleterious, not to say immoral; and for the future, I am sternly resolved to rise at seven o'clock, and have my tea and toast in a decent breakfast-parlor punctually at eight. Good-bye, ladies and gentlemen; may your shadows and digestions never be less. Good-bye, Hircius and Spungius, engaging "Companions of my Solitude," inexhaustible themes for "Essays written in the intervals of Business." Farewell, my best beloved; we may meet again,

shortly. I take my leave with feelings of affection towards all the world—feelings that o'er-
brim my eyes and swell my bosom. What are
riches, honors, dignities? Give me HEART!
Bless everybody!

THE END.